RIVER OF INK
IMMORTAL

HELEN DENNIS

Illustrated by
BONNIE KATE WOLF

Hodder
Children's
Books

HODDER CHILDREN'S BOOKS

First published in Great Britain in 2017 by Hodder and Stoughton

1 3 5 7 9 10 8 6 4 2

A CIP catalogue record for this book is available from the British Library.

ISBN: 978 1 444 92049 9

Typeset in Adobe Garamond by Avon DataSet Ltd, Bidford-on-Avon, Warwickshire

Printed in Great Britain by Clays Ltd, St Ives plc

The paper and board used in this book are made from wood from responsible sources.

Hodder Children's Books
An imprint of Hachette Children's Group
Part of Hodder and Stoughton
Carmelite House
50 Victoria Embankment
London EC4Y 0DZ

An Hachette UK Company
www.hachette.co.uk

www.hachettechildrens.co.uk

For
everyday heroes everywhere

'It is nothing to die; it is frightful not to live.'

– Victor Hugo

DAY 299

In the night, snow had fallen. It had covered everything, shrouding the desert and transforming it. Nothing looked like it had done before. It was hard to tell what was alive, and what was dead.

Rock poked through the snow like fingers. Tree branches looked like arms forced into thick woollen jumpers. Birds huddled together, and none of them sang.

The river was a mirror of ice. It no longer flowed, as if time, like the water, had been frozen.

But Jed knew that time hadn't stopped. His heart raced and the scars scorched across his chest pulsed with pain.

Jed knelt beside the river. From far off it might have looked as if he was praying, though he said nothing. His hands rested on the ice. The cold burned

1

him and he did not pull away.

Suddenly, from the window sill of the church in the rock behind him, a bird flapped her wings and rose into the air. Her feet and feathers sent snow tumbling. As Jed turned his head, he thought the falling snow looked like smoke. A phoenix rising from white, hot flames.

The bird circled above him, writing her route across the sky. And then, even though Jed scrunched up his eyes to see her, she became blurred, just a smudge in the clouds.

Jed turned back to face the river. He pressed his palm on to the skin of snow that covered the ice. His reflection swam into view like a boy rising from the depths and fighting to be free. The face he saw seemed unfamiliar, distorted by the cracks and bubbles in the ice.

Jed drew his hands back. He had no idea who the boy in the river was any more. He had no idea what to do or where to go. Anger boiled inside him. He flung his arm behind his head and drove his fist into the ice. The surface cracked and splintered like glass. The boy in the river disintegrated, then disappeared. Jed's fingers plunged into the water. Cold scalded deep into his skin. A tiny streak of blood swirled free from a reopened gash in his palm, eddying in a circle on the surface of the water, before it diluted then disappeared like the reflection.

He pulled his hand free and held it to his chest. Blood from the cut in his life-line leaked on to his shirt. He rubbed his wrist, then dug around in his trouser pocket for something to wrap around his wound. A large, silver watch fell from his pocket.

Kassia had given him the watch back in London, when the adventure had been just beginning. It had belonged to her father.

Jed felt his insides turn to water, churning like the broken river.

Jed had been there the day Kassia's dad had died. It had been his fault. He had told her that, when they'd stood together inside the Dark Church in Karanlik Kilise, Turkey, barely thirteen days ago. She had looked at him and anger had raged behind her eyes, scaring him in the same way as he was scared now by his own reflection.

She and Dante had left. By now they would be back in London. And he was here in Turkey. Alone.

Blood trickled slowly on to the casing of the pocket watch. A single swallow was engraved on the back, its wings thrown wide in flight.

Jed looked up to the sky again. He could no longer see the bird from the church. The phoenix was gone.

When water gets colder than 32 degrees Fahrenheit or zero degrees
it freezes into ice. As the water gets colder, the molecules of water
energy and move more slowly - that's why the molecules become cold
molecules move more slowly, it is easier for them to hook on to
sharing electrons. When enough of the molecules hook on to

And so there it was again. The same thought spinning back to him. Kassia was in London, hating him for what he'd done. And Jed was here. Hating himself.

He took a deep breath, pushed the watch into his pocket, then wrapped his injured hand awkwardly with a tissue.

The water in the river had settled. No longer frozen where he'd driven his hand through the surface, but calm and still. And his reflection had returned.

He might not understand who the boy in the river was. But he knew that staying would solve nothing.

He turned and walked carefully across the snow, seeking out the path that led away from here.

He knew now that the time had come.

DAY 300

24th December

It was raining when the plane landed at Heathrow. The sky was mottled grey and closing in, making it look like it had been shrunk by all the water.

The pavements were puddled. Cars were driving as fast as ever, spraying pedestrians with dirt from the gutters, while cyclists wobbled and wove in the wake of big red buses. A black taxi screeched to a standstill as an elderly man and lady tottered on the edge of the kerb, arms extended painfully by bulging shopping bags. Tinny music pumped from shop doors and strips of electric lighting flashed white above them, as if the solar system had been dragged down by all the rain and re-strung between the shop fronts of London.

'It's nearly Christmas,' said Kassia in sign language, turning her face away from the driving rain and moving her fingers as quickly as the cold would allow. 'I'd forgotten.'

'Thought you'd forgotten how to talk, too,' signed Dante. 'You've barely said anything since Istanbul.'

Kassia shrugged. 'There's nothing to say.'

'Really? No reason? No brief summary about why we *had* to come home? After everything we've been through?'

'Not yet,' Kassia signed. 'I can't explain it all twice.'

It was her brother's turn to shrug. 'Are you sure you're ready for this?' They'd turned the corner of Fleet Street. The door to the flat they'd both grown up in was visible.

'It looks the same,' Kassia signed tentatively. She knew this didn't make any sense. The whole flat had been gutted by a fire just after Easter. But the rebuild was impressive. It looked just as it had. Maybe the paint was a fraction duller. Though this didn't seem possible. Their mum had a thing about cleanliness. She'd washed the old door with carbolic soap at least once a week.

Kassia shivered. And it wasn't from the cold.

Supposing things were just as they'd been? Her mum would be so cross. Kassia and Dante had been away for months with hardly any contact with Mum or Uncle Nat. Any discussions had been via email and even those had been in code. The organisation which went by the name of NOAH had been tracking their every move since they'd got involved with Jed. In fact, NOAH had been responsible for the fire that destroyed the flat, although the insurance company claimed it was started by faulty hair-straighteners. The truth was, though, knowing that NOAH would stop at nothing to catch them meant that any messages sent back home were at risk of being intercepted. So they'd tried not to take many risks. The last message had been from Paris, and that felt a lifetime ago.

Dante moved his hands in sign again and Kassia realised that she must look nervous. 'Are you sure you're ready?'

Kassia nodded.

Dante took a key and fumbled it in the keyhole. He shook his head and dropped the key back into his pocket. 'New lock,' he said. 'Obvious. Brand new door.'

Kassia nodded again, with a little less confidence.

Dante pressed the doorbell.

There was no sound. But the lights flashed off inside the flat.

Kassia watched Dante's reaction. It was clear he hadn't been expecting this. The old system of alerting deaf people to the arrival of visitors using light instead of sound had been his dad's idea. And Kassia guessed her brother had expected that in the rebuild this feature would have been dropped. His mum must have asked for it, Kassia thought, and this made her feel strangely lightheaded.

Kassia reached out and pulled her brother's finger off the doorbell. The lights flashed back on.

So things *were* just as they had been. Kassia stood up straight, trying to make herself look brave. Nothing had changed.

But when the front door opened, it was clear that everything *had* changed.

Their mother, Anna, stood there. She leant her weight against the doorjamb as if the door was holding her up. As if she would melt and flow away into the puddles on the pavement if she let go.

Her hair was scraped away from her face, tied tight in a ponytail, but tendrils curled loose, untamed, wispy and wild.

Deep lines ran from the edges of her eyes. Time had clearly been scoring a space on which to write.

Anna's mouth opened and closed. But no sounds came.

Then she crumpled to her knees.

And Kassia knelt down too, half in the entrance to the flat and half in the street, and it didn't matter that the rain soaked her legs or lashed down on her shoulders, because her mum was holding her and breathing into her hair in long, spluttering sobs and reaching out for her brother who sank to his knees beside them. Three figures bowed down in a doorway in the fading light of Christmas Eve.

For the first time since leaving Turkey, Kassia allowed herself to cry.

DAY 301
~25th December

Kassia sat on the end of her bed. She supposed it *was* her bed because it was in the room that used to be hers. But this room looked nothing like it had before the fire.

The walls were bare of timetables. There were no charts or schedules. Instead, there was a neatly framed picture of the sea pinned to one side of the lilac room, and a fan of peacock feathers attached to the other. There were no stacks of school books or revision guides. There were fairy lights around the headboard and a dream catcher hanging at the window.

It *did* look like her room. But not her room here. It was like her room in her dad's house in Spain.

Anna stood in the doorway. She held a plate in her hand, smiled and put it on the cabinet beside the bed. On the plate were chocolate biscuits.

Kassia twisted her fingers together in an attempt to hide her surprise, then looked down at the carpet. It was purple, flecked with small pink flowers. 'The room's beautiful,' Kassia mumbled.

Her mum sat down beside her.

'So are you,' Anna said, gazing towards the carpet too. Kassia noticed that her mum was wearing outside shoes. 'I missed you both so much.'

Her mum looked fleetingly at Dante, who was in a chair by the window, and then repeated her words in sign. The next sentence was muddled and flustered as her fingers tried to keep up with the words from her mouth. 'I hoped and hoped that you would be back for Christmas and I just thought if maybe there was a way to . . .' She reached for the plate of biscuits and thrust them towards Dante.

He took one but Anna held the plate in front of him, so he took another and balanced them on his knees so his hands were free to sign. 'That's enough chocolate, Mum. Thanks. Don't want to shock the system.'

Kassia watched her mum stare at him, as if checking he was really there.

'You put up a Christmas tree,' Kassia said quietly. 'Bought us presents.'

Her mum nodded. 'I thought if I kept believing . . .'

Kassia felt her stomach clench. 'In Christmas?'

'In you. That you'd come back.'

The knot in Kassia's stomach tightened. Something that felt like guilt pressed hard around her throat. Everything was so confused. Nothing about this day was like Christmases from before, and yet . . .

She watched as her mum held the plate of biscuits in her hands. Chocolate in her bedroom. Fairy lights. Sitting together early Christmas morning. Maybe it was like Christmases from the past after all. But ones long ago, before her dad had died. Before Christmas had been an interruption to a work schedule.

From somewhere outside, Kassia could hear Christmas music playing.

'It was so complicated,' Kassia blurted. 'There wasn't time to tell you.'

The plate of biscuits wobbled as Anna placed it back on the cabinet. 'Tell me now. Tell me everything.'

And so Kassia did.

She explained about Jed.

She talked about him climbing out of the River Thames, on a clear day at the very end of February. She went over how he couldn't remember who he was, or why he was in the river. And then she told her mum about the missing part of the story and what he'd finally remembered.

14

He was an alchemist.

Not a modern one, messing about with chemicals in test-tubes in some fancy modern laboratory. But a real alchemist. From over a hundred years ago.

Of course he didn't look this old. He'd used alchemy to make the elixir of life and it had worked. It had made his whole system do a kind of rebooting. This happened sometimes in nature, with things like jellyfish, Kassia added, when her mum looked totally horrified. Kassia agreed it was more than a little weird with humans. *Linear reprogramming*, it was called, and it had taken Jed's body back to an earlier version of himself. The memories of all he'd been and all he'd done before had been lost. But they had gradually returned.

Kassia faltered here, her words so quiet that it was really only her hands that were talking.

But Anna urged her to go on, her eyes narrowed as if maybe if she focused hard enough then what Kassia was saying would make some sort of sense.

Kassia explained that the whole elixir thing had been the reason NOAH were after Jed. A National Organisation concerned with 'Absolute Health' saw him as the answer. A way of getting the recipe for immortality. Their plan was to sell the secret to the highest bidder. They would be in control, then, of who lived and who died. The ultimate elixir would give them ultimate power.

Except Jed didn't remember how to make it.

And that wasn't only a problem for NOAH.

There was a catch with how the elixir worked. It had to be taken six times to make the transformation of Jed's body complete. He'd only taken the elixir five times. He needed one more dose. And he needed it quickly. Before the last day of February, in fact.

'Why then?' cut in Anna.

'He climbed out of the Thames on the last day of February. He must take the elixir before he reaches that date again. Midnight. February the twenty-seventh. That's when the year is up.' Kassia's signing faltered now.

Anna looked across at Dante. 'And if he doesn't take the elixir within a year?' she signed, her eyes still narrowed, the lines at their edges deep.

'Jed will die.'

The three of them sat in silence for a moment. Kassia watched the dreamcatcher sway slightly in the draught from the window. Dante put down his half-eaten biscuit.

'So we had to find the recipe,' Kassia signed at last.

'All this time, you've been looking?' Anna asked.

'Looking. And trying to get away from NOAH.'

Kassia saw her mother bristle. 'But we did come really close to the recipe.'

'Not close enough?'

Kassia shook her head. 'Jed was getting ill. I guess his body was desperate for the sixth elixir. He started to remember things. From before.'

Dante leant forward, clearly sensing that now was the time for the real explanations about why they were home.

'He remembered the days he'd taken the elixir,' Kassia said. 'And one of the days was in 2003.'

Anna's confusion matched that written across Dante's face, but Kassia ploughed on.

'A particular day in 2003. The day Dad died.'

Kassia could see that Dante's jaw was tightening. She didn't stop.

'Jed was there. And Dad's death was Jed's fault.'

Dante bolted from the chair, his hands pitched wide, scratching through the air to find the signs he needed. But the only sign he found was the one for 'Dad'. His fingers banged against each other again and again, making the word over and over.

'I couldn't tell you in Turkey,' Kassia pleaded. 'I couldn't get my head round it. I needed to get away.'

'Dad?' Dante signed again.

Anna stood up too and took Dante's hands and

held them apart so the signing stopped. But the word hung between them, as it always had.

Kassia swallowed her sobs. The dreamcatcher struck the glass of the window, like fingers rapping to be heard.

Anna steered Dante back towards the chair and eased him down. She knelt between her son and daughter and for a moment she held on to them both so that they were joined in a chain.

Then Anna released their hands to sign. 'Did Jed crash your father's car?'

'No. Dad was driving after Jed.' Kassia's answer fumbled through her fingers. 'But if Jed hadn't been in trouble, Dad wouldn't have been following him.'

'Did Jed mean your dad harm?'

Again, Kassia's fingers stuttered on the words she made. 'I'm not sure.' Then she shook her head, remembering the story. 'No. He didn't mean to hurt him.'

'So the crash was an accident?'

'No!' Kassia signed indignantly. 'Dad was shot at!'

'By Jed?'

'By NOAH.'

Anna wiped her face with the back of her hand. Kassia could see her mum's fingers were wet as she carried on signing. 'So the people who harmed your father were the ones who wanted to harm Jed? But you're blaming him?'

Kassia looked at the floor again. The pink flowers swam in and out of focus behind her tears.

'Kassia?' her mum said gently.

'Jed shouldn't have been there,' Kassia blurted defensively. 'It's *all* connected. A giant loop, like the ouroboros, and it all leads back to Jed.'

'And that makes him to blame?' signed Anna.

'No. But . . .'

Anna sat up. She looked first at Dante and then Kassia but her signs were directed to the space in between them, as if she wanted there to be no chance that either of them would misunderstand. 'Your dad was a good man.'

Dante's hands shot forward in answer. 'You stopped speaking to him! You made him move out!'

Anna stared at her own fingers, watching her words so she would make them clearer. 'Life is complicated. It's not clear and uncluttered. There aren't always just good and bad decisions. Your father and I disagreed.'

'About me?' Dante's hands shouted.

'Yes! Amongst other things. Life was hard for a while and we had the chance to make it right. But things went wrong.'

'What are you saying?' Kassia said.

Anna shook her hands as if her fingers were cramping and the signing hurt her. But she carried on, slowly forming each word. 'The fire destroyed everything here. Our plans. Our timetables. All the things I thought were important. But there was one box. Jed found it, I think, in your wardrobe, on the day he started speaking.'

'The box of things from before Dad left? Pictures I'd made? My stories?'

Anna nodded.

'But the fire burnt *everything*?'

'Everything in the flat,' said Anna slowly. 'I was angry. That Jed had seen that stuff and so I took the box and I gave it to Nat. To get rid of. But he didn't. It was at his house before the fire. So it survived. That box was all I had left.'

Kassia remembered the contents of the box. Childhood paintings, a plasticine tortoise, a paper snowflake. All stuff from before the timetable and the charts that Mum had become obsessed with after Dad left.

'I promised myself,' Anna went on, 'that if you and Dante ever came back, I'd do all I could to make things better. That *whatever* happened in the past, we'd make the future right again. Time is so precious.'

Kassia folded her arms across herself and she was

surprised to find she was shaking. Maybe from exhaustion; maybe from the shock of being back after so long away; or maybe something else.

Silence lengthened between them, before Anna moved to sit on the end of the bed. Kassia sighed, then because she had no idea what to do next, she laid her head on her mother's lap. She hadn't done that for years. She closed her eyes as her mother smoothed her fingers through her hair. The only sound was the noise of the rain. And the dreamcatcher's gentle clicking on the windowpane like the ticking of a clock.

'Sometimes,' her mum said quietly, 'there are things you cannot change. You just have to change the ones you can.'

Time was precious. Jed had only weeks left to find the elixir. But it was too late now.

Even if Kassia wanted to change things, Jed was half a world away.

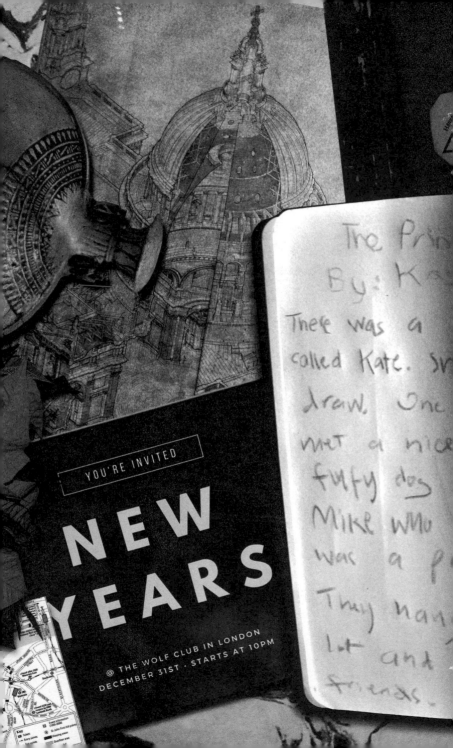

they are in a park playing fetch when an evil witch banishes Kim from the park! She gets a new place called RED bridge and then are so forced so she sends a letter to Mike to lead him to her with clues so they watch everything

DAY 307
31st December

Reverend Solomon Cockren, the chaplain at St Paul's Cathedral in London, slammed the book down on the end of the large oak table. The noise echoed round the library. The Wren Library was rarely used. And the ornate room, ringed by huge wooden shelves loaded with leather-backed books, was rarely accustomed to such noise. 'Enough is enough,' he growled.

Victor, a boy with buzz cut hair and eyes the colour of spilt oil, pressed his hands heavily on the discarded book. 'You think you've told me enough!' he snarled. 'You haven't told me anything! I need to know about my father! You promised to tell me all there was to know about Orin Sinclair.'

Reverend Cockren spun round. The edge of his cassock fanned in the air like huge black wings, and the white stole around his neck flapped behind him.

'I've made a lot of promises, Victor. Some are harder to keep than others!' He paced backwards and forwards, the stole a streak of white on either side of his arms. 'Sometimes the weight of the work of one's father is a heavy burden to bear!'

'You're not making any sense!' the teenage boy snapped at him.

'Well, maybe life is just one big riddle.'

Victor's forehead wrinkled in contempt as he swept the discarded book from the end of the table and on to the floor. It splayed open, its pages creasing and crumpling as it fell.

'You have to give me time!' groaned Reverend Cockren. 'I have to be sure I can trust you!'

Victor stood up straight, his arms spread wide in surrender. 'You can trust me!' he shouted.

Reverend Cockren reached for the boy's arm, and pushed up the sleeve of his shirt to reveal a tattoo of a unicorn in chains. 'Really? You live with NOAH? You wear their mark! How can I trust you?'

Victor tugged his arm away, grabbed his coat from the back of a chair and stormed towards the door. 'I will be back, old man,' he yelled. 'I am risking everything to see you. They cannot know I've been here.'

'So maybe I need proof of your loyalty!' Reverend

Cockren called after him.

Victor shook his head as he hurried down the stairs from the library and out into the main body of the cathedral. Reverend Cockren followed, trying desperately to keep up. Then he took a key and hastily opened a side door and ushered the boy into the street outside.

'You understand that NOAH don't work alone, don't you?' the Reverend muttered. 'If I anger them, I upset people in very high places.'

Victor looked skyward, as if the chaplain was making reference to an otherworldly power.

'People in government,' snapped Reverend Cockren. 'NOAH doesn't do what it does alone.'

As Victor turned away, the Reverend blurted, 'I need time to be sure which side you're on.'

Victor spun round. 'Time is running out!' he snarled.

Reverend Cockren raised his hand to touch the boy's shoulder, but Victor shrugged it away and pulled his coat around his shoulders. He turned his head into the biting cold and hurried down the steps, taking them two at a time, glancing back only once before he strode off in the direction of the river.

Reverend Cockren turned the key over and over in his hand. The metal was cold against his skin.

There were few people outside and those that were ignored the enormous building looming down on them. Most were in London to celebrate. Early revellers who wanted the best view of the firework display to mark the end of one year and the start of a new. The chaplain used to play a game when he stood on the steps of the cathedral. He tried to guess the stories of those who hurried past him and the game would amuse him. Now there was no fun in it. He'd learnt that people's stories were so much more complicated than the tale that could be seen on the surface.

As Reverend Cockren turned, he noticed three people walking closely together, away from the direction taken by those striding towards the river. A teenage girl, who was clutching a bunch of flowers, her mother, perhaps, and an older boy. There was something familiar about them.

The girl stopped, for just a second. She looked up at the cathedral and her face, flushed by the cold of the day, suddenly darkened as a shadow moved across it.

Reverend Solomon scuffed his feet against the ground, kicking back through his memories. He struggled to place the girl, but the image blazed frustratingly. There was something about her. Something he recognised. Before he could locate her amongst all the faces in his mind, he saw something

27

else. On the other side of the steps, hidden from the view of the girl with the flowers, a red-headed boy looked towards the door.

No searching in his memory was needed to remember this face. It was the boy from the river. He was staring at the cathedral as he had done all those months ago, lost and afraid.

Reverend Cockren stumbled back inside, slammed the side door and fumbled with the key. He leant against the wall, waiting for his heartbeat to slow.

It didn't.

It was still racing when the chaplain reached his office.

He fumbled in his desk drawer, rummaging through leaflets and rejected sermon notes, until he found what he was looking for.

A tiny notebook with a thick, black cardboard cover. A circle, a square and a triangle had been branded on the front. Another mark. Not for NOAH. This time the mark was for the Brothers of Heliopolis.

Reverend Cockren flicked through the pages, scanning the names. Many had been scored through, rewritten or substituted with alternatives. The name he needed was written in green ink across the top of a clean page. It was an unusual name for a Frenchman. It sounded more like the name of a clown.

Reverend Cockren put the book on the desk beside the telephone. Then he lifted the receiver and very carefully, sounding out each number aloud, he dialled.

The number 101 bus pulled to a halt in front of the entrance to the City of London Cemetery and Crematorium.

'Mind as you go, now,' said the driver, as the last few passengers shambled down the steps and on to the pavement. 'Happy New Year to you all,' he called, in a way that made Kassia think perhaps his shift was over now and he was more than a little looking forward to the midnight celebrations. 'And don't you all go forgetting,' the driver added, 'that it's bank holiday service tomorrow, so make sure you check the Sunday timetable!' He belly-laughed. 'Although of course I'm thinking there's a fair to middling chance yous lot will spend tomorrow kipping, sleeping off your partying.'

Kassia thought this an odd comment to make to a group of passengers being dropped off at a graveyard, but from the way the driver pulled the bus away from the kerb and headed towards the depot, she supposed it was his own need for sleep tomorrow he was really thinking about.

Kassia tightened her grip on the bunch of huge red poinsettias they'd got from the florist. They were beautiful, although there were one or two browned petals around the edge of the bunch, probably because the driver had insisted on turning the heater on the bus up to full power. She fidgeted awkwardly with the shrivelled petals, hoping to catch them before her mum noticed. But Anna tapped her hand gently. 'They're perfect,' she said.

Kassia left the brown petals where they were. She wasn't sure she'd ever heard her mum use that word before. Unless she was adding the words 'not' or 'far from' in front of it. It sounded odd all on its own.

The three of them made their way along the central avenue of the cemetery. The crowd who had got off the bus at the same time as them thinned away gradually, making their way towards various graves and ornamental angels. By the time the three of them reached the turning for their father's grave, they were the only ones left on the main path.

Dante stopped short of the gravestone.

Kassia noticed instantly that the border of the grass between the headstone and the slab on the ground was a little high. She looked up at her mum. Anna said nothing. Not to them, at any rate, although Kassia was sure she heard her whisper something towards the grave.

Her mother never spoke to her dad. They'd been

through that. There was no need to start talking to him after he'd died when she'd given up conversation with him while he was alive, and yet Kassia was sure her mother was muttering something gently.

Then her mother did something else Kassia had never seen her do. She knelt beside the grave and lifted a bunch of wilting flowers from the vase at the base. Who had brought those flowers? Her mum? Last week? But she ... .

Kassia froze.

Suddenly, it was no longer important.

Kassia reached out her free hand to clutch Dante and then pointed.

There was a single orange rose lying on the top of her dad's headstone.

Kassia dropped the bunch of poinsettias and darted forward to pick up the rose. 'It's Jed! It's Jed!' she babbled.

Dante laughed as he signed his answer. 'Well, it kind of isn't Jed, is it?' he mocked. 'It's a rose.'

Kassia waved the single stem in front of him and tried to answer, although holding the rose made signing so awkward she had to drop it again. 'Jed left the rose,' she scrambled with her fingers.

'Now hold on,' signed Dante, looking a little more serious. 'It could just be a Christmas or New

Year thing. You know, that the staff here do. A kind of nice gesture, which no doubt we pay for in our ground fees.'

Kassia waved her hands wildly. 'Do you see any other single orange roses? On any other graves except this one?'

Dante took a while to answer, humouring her by looking around. 'Well, no. But Jed's in Turkey,' he signed, as if she was a very young child and couldn't possibly be expected to follow the conversation. 'What makes you think that Jed could be the one who put the rose here?'

'It's orange!'

Dante stared sharply at her, making it clear that simply relying on the colour choice wasn't a good enough answer.

Their mum leant forward, grabbing his hands in an attempt to interrupt. 'Orange is the colour of hope,' she said.

'I told Jed that once.' Kassia nodded enthusiastically. 'He's been here. I know he has.'

Kassia watched her mum and Dante exchange glances. Dante certainly didn't need to use signs to make it clear what he was thinking.

'Supposing he has come back,' Kassia ploughed on. 'And—'

'I thought it was over.' It was Dante's turn to interrupt. 'I thought, after all you said. After knowing what you did, then . . .' He stalled.

Kassia looked across at her mum. Anna knew orange meant hope. And her mum *had* said all that stuff about changing all the things you could when Kassia had told Jed's story. 'But if he's back,' Kassia signed cautiously, 'and if the rose is from him, then don't you think he could be trying to say he's sorry?'

Dante flung his arms towards the sky. 'You're impossible, Kass! We went across the world for Jed. We lived underground for him, risked all we had for him. And it was you – ' his hands were raging now – 'it was you,' he said again, 'who gave up on him. You were the one who let him go.'

'Maybe I was wrong. Maybe it's all much more complicated.'

Dante's signs were enormous. His arms couldn't stretch any further to contain them. 'Complicated! That doesn't even come close to what this is!'

Anna got up from her knees, last week's flowers and the new poinsettias mixing in a muddled mess on the gravestone. 'So maybe it *should* be simple.'

Dante stared at her.

'While you were both gone,' she said, 'and after everything got lost in the fire, I realised that I'd been

33

fighting so long and so hard to be in control. I wanted to force what *was* into something new,' Anna went on. 'Maybe I should have just tried to move on with what happened and let life run its course.'

This was too much for Kassia. What had happened to her mother? And what had any of this got to do with Jed and the very real possibility that he was back in London?

'You seem to have done a *lot* of thinking while we were away,' signed Dante.

'When you lose what's important to you, it makes you think about what means most,' said Anna. 'It's like I told you on Christmas Day. When Nat gave me the box of things you'd made when you were young, it all clicked somehow. They were the only things that survived the fire. And I realised then that it wasn't the timetables, or even the flat that meant most. It was being with you two.'

Kassia didn't know what to say. She reached down for the rose. 'Mum, we kind of noticed things have changed for you. But what does this mean for us?'

'I think you need to ask yourself what you want,' Anna said quietly, 'now that you've lost everything.'

Kassia looked at the rose. The edges of the petals overlapped in a tight and perfect circle so it was difficult to see the end or the beginning of the ring. 'If

Jed is back in London,' she said, the rose now moving effortlessly with her hands as they signed, 'I want to see him.'

'London's a big place,' signed Dante. 'If he's really back, he could be anywhere.'

Kassia turned the thought over in her head. She gripped the stem of the orange rose tight between her fingers. 'I know where he'll be,' she said.

Victor Sinclair was lying on his bed. The novelty he felt about his bedroom in The Shard building, right in the centre of London and overlooking the River Thames, never got old. When NOAH had first brought him to live with them nearly a year ago, and rescued him from the nightmare care home, Etkin House, where he'd been forced to live since his parents had died, he couldn't believe it was possible to stay anywhere so posh. It still seemed like this should belong in someone else's life, and he wondered if he'd ever really feel at home here.

He gazed at the poster of the constellations stuck to the ceiling and tried to breathe deeply. He'd heard this deep breathing business was a good way of coping with anger and stress.

It wasn't working. He was still mad. Why would no one, anywhere, *ever* give him any straight answers?

He threw a tennis ball at the ceiling. It landed somewhere between Orion's Belt and the edge of the Plough like it had done the last hundred or so times he'd thrown it up there. The paper of the poster was beginning to wear away from the repeated bashing and it made it look as if the light of the stars was fading.

Suddenly, there was a knock at the door. Victor jumped and the tennis ball landed squarely on his nose on its return descent from the stars. He swallowed a string of swear words as his eyes smarted with the pain.

Brilliant. Now he was angry, confused *and* had a broken nose. Could this day get any better?

He sat up on the bed as a thought dawned on him. The day could certainly get *worse* if the person beyond the door doing the knocking was Cole Carter. Victor rubbed his face as the knocking came again.

'All right, all right, I'm coming!' he mumbled. If it was Cole, Victor would send him away. There was no way he was traipsing off anywhere today with someone who used more hair products than the entire cast of *Hairspray* the musical put together, and insisted on wearing a long, black leather coat whether it was snowing outside or over ninety degrees. Victor wasn't in the mood to go looking for the guy NOAH called the unicorn. If this Jed/Fulcanelli/River Boy person, or whatever he called himself, had really worked out how to live for ever, then Victor and Cole had all the time in the world to catch him up. Victor had his own issues to deal with.

Sure, Cole had been kind of supportive in the beginning. And maybe racing across Europe, flinging themselves off moving trains and charging around in the sewers of Paris had been fun for a while. But he and Cole hadn't had the best success rate. Montgomery, their boss, was far from happy and so if Cole had come here with travel plans that involved hot air balloon races in Turkey or anything wild like that, Victor was going to make a stand, because it was time they came up with a proper strategy.

Victor was going to say *all this* as he opened the door.

Except the person doing the knocking wasn't Cole Carter.

'Oh,' said Victor. He rubbed the tears from his eyes and was suddenly aware that if his nose hurt as much as it did, there was a very high chance it would be red, which would probably not be his greatest look.

The security guard who worked in the lifts in The Shard stood in the corridor. He winced sympathetically and then, suddenly aware that staring at someone's nose wasn't the politest thing in the world, he looked down at the carpet.

'Oh, of course,' Victor said quickly, turning from the door and marching across the room towards the mini-bar. He'd used chocolate to get round these guys before when he'd first arrived in the building and he was pretty sure the guards and lift attendants were working on a rota to get the stuff from here when there were gaps in their work schedule.

But the security guard called out behind him. 'I'm not here for chocolate,' he said quickly. 'Wife's got me on a post-Christmas no sugar, no carb diet. Not allowed anything that tastes good, either,' he mumbled resentfully.

'Oh.' Victor stopped midway across the room and turned to face the guard.

'I've got a special delivery,' the man explained.

Victor never got post. There was no one to write to him. He had no family and the staff at Etkin House hadn't sent him a birthday or Christmas card in all the years he'd lived there so there was no chance that anyone there would be writing to him.

He took the small brown envelope from the security guard and then groaned gently as the raising of his eyebrows he made to signal his surprise sent shooting pains through his nose. 'Who's it from?' he said. 'Montgomery? Martha Quinn? They're not chucking me out, are they?'

Victor had been thinking recently that whatever agreement the heads of department at NOAH had made with his dad to take him in when he was the right age, might have had a let-out clause in it. He'd failed to catch Fulcanelli for them. And that was all they'd asked him to do. Maybe this was the way they booted him out. A letter instead of a face-to-face confrontation, in case things got really awkward.

'It's external mail,' the security guard explained.

'Oh.' Victor didn't know what to say. He held the envelope in his hand as the guard turned and made his way out of the door.

Victor sat on the bed. He put the envelope beside him and for a few minutes he didn't look at it. The tennis ball was on the floor between his feet, unmoving.

Victor looked up again at the star chart. He kicked the tennis ball under his bed, got up and strode towards the mini-bar. If the guard didn't want the chocolate then he certainly did.

He downed the whole bar in barely more than three bites. Then he walked slowly back over to the bed, lifted the envelope and very carefully slipped his finger under the seal.

There was a single piece of paper inside.

Victor stood under fading paper stars as he read it.

* * *

It was getting dark. But London had no intention of going to sleep. People spilt out of restaurants and cafés, stepped out of black taxis and off red buses and surged from underground stations, bubbling up as if from underground streams. The crowd was moving as one in the direction of the Thames.

Kassia battled against them, swimming upstream.

Her mum had made her read an article a few years ago about salmon and how they fought their way against the current to go the wrong way up rivers. Apparently, they did this to get to the place where they'd been born. Her mum had made a big thing about the salmon's resilience and determination to achieve its goal. But what had struck Kassia about the article was the idea of where the fish was trying to get to. Home.

She stumbled awkwardly against the edge of the kerb and then steadied herself to elbow her way through a group of middle-aged women who were dressed in tutu skirts and sporting clip-on fairy wings. The women wobbled about so much in their pink high heels it was pretty clear they'd struggle to be capable of even standing by the time midnight came round.

'Oi, watch yourself!' one woman shouted, waving a fairy wand at Kassia. The wand was bent into the shape of banana, which made Kassia think that at some point on the journey one of the larger fairies must have sat on it.

A car blasted its horn as another horde of people ignored the red pedestrian traffic signal and strode over the crossing regardless. A teenage girl thrust a leaflet into Kassia's hand. It offered ten per cent off an all-day breakfast between two and four in the morning in some café next to Ye Olde Cheshire Cheese Pub in Fleet Street, as well as promotional information about historic buildings that were staying open late as part of the New Year celebrations. Kassia scrunched the voucher into a ball. She shook her head at another woman who was wearing a hi-vis jacket and offering packets of disposable earplugs wrapped in flyers about firework safety.

Kassia ploughed on.

Her feet thudded the pavements. The air was so bitter it hurt her throat. Her eyes stung from the wind.

Her mum and Dante had wanted to come. But Kassia hadn't given them time to argue and so they had only accompanied her as far as Fleet Street.

She knew where she was going. She wanted to do this last bit alone.

Postman's Park was a quiet part of London at the best of times. And on this day, when time was running out and a brand new calendar year was just about to start, it was even quieter than usual.

There were no office workers catching a quick break between high-powered boardroom meetings. There were no fitness experts shadow-boxing or practising Tai Chi. There weren't even any tourists grabbing quick photos of the Watt's Memorial to Heroic Self-Sacrifice before heading off round the corner to squeeze in a quick visit to the Museum of London. Even the pigeons that usually speckled the grass hoping for a stolen feast were huddled together in the trees trying desperately to keep warm.

The sun was long gone. The only light came from street lamps. There was no moon.

Kassia caught her breath and the eerie silence of the garden stole over her.

She couldn't hear the crowds rushing for the river or even the traffic funnelling along King Edward Street. Only the sound of her heartbeat throbbing in her ears.

She hesitated for a moment, before stepping quietly towards the memorial.

Electric lighting flickered under the wooden canopy that stuck out from the far end of the park, protecting the decorated plaques that lined the wall. Kassia had been here so many times that she knew many of the stories behind the plaques off by heart: Alice Ayres, who saved three children from a burning house; Elizabeth Boxall, who saved a child from a runaway horse; and Arthur Strange and Mark Tomlinson, who saved two girls from quicksand.

But tonight things did not feel familiar.

Kassia peered into the far corner of the memorial. Old headstones from the church had been propped here against the wall. Someone was crouching in front of them.

Nearly a year ago, Kassia had found Jed in the same place, crouched like this, his back pressed against the graves. For a moment then, she hadn't known who he was. Now, she knew.

His head was down and he was clutching his knees, pulled tight against his chest.

She walked slowly towards him, and even though she walked on grass, she was sure her footsteps echoed, like the hands of a clock ticking down the minutes until midnight.

'Jed?' she said gently.

He looked up at her.

Without really meaning to, she let the orange rose she carried tumble from her hand.

The rose rocked backwards and forwards on the ground between them and a single petal came free and blew away on the wind.

Jed scrambled to his knees. 'You found it. You found . . .' – his voice trailed away – '. . . me.'

Kassia nodded. She wasn't sure what to say and she wasn't sure anyway that her voice was still working. There was a thickening across her throat and the sound of her heartbeat was so loud in her ears that Jed's voice was distorted.

Jed reached out and helped as she sank to her knees, turning her slightly so that her back pressed against the gravestones for support. 'Here, let me . . .' He was mumbling, his words incoherent and breathy.

He watched as her breathing settled, his eyes narrowed under the flicker of the electric lighting. But even now she had no idea what to say.

It had been nearly a month since she'd walked away from him in Turkey. There had been no big goodbye. She hadn't given him the chance for that. He'd told her what he'd remembered about things that happened on the day he'd taken the fifth dose of the elixir. And then she'd left. That was it. Now there was all this unsaid stuff between them and she hadn't got a clue where to start.

'Erm, I should . . .' Her throat closed up again and she said nothing more. Instead she stared at him and tried to work out what he was thinking. His face looked more lined than it had, the skin paler, the freckles darker, heavier even below his eyes, and she was scared to try and read what she saw.

They sat for a while in the silence of the memorial.

Finally, he turned his face so that he couldn't see her response and he whispered quietly, 'I really do want to be someone worth saving.'

'I know,' she said.

They sat, then, for even longer without speaking, though the silence felt less awkward than it had.

'My mum thinks I should give you another chance,' Kassia said eventually.

Jed moved his head so that he was facing her and this time he did not look away. 'Your *mum* does?'

'She did this whole big thing,' Kassia went on, 'about coping with things as they are now.'

Jed's eyes seemed to flicker and Kassia thought that what she saw in them might be hope.

'That doesn't mean I can forget about you being there when my dad died,' she added. 'It doesn't mean I can get my head round all the things you did in the past.' In those final moments in Turkey he hadn't just told her about the last day of the elixir. He'd explained new ways of seeing the other memories that he'd had. The truth of who he really was and what he'd really done – and why – had hurt her.

'But what it does mean, is . . .' Now the hope was

even more obvious. She took a deep breath. The gravestone was cold against her back but she knew it was supporting her. 'I guess this thing is so complicated that I want to see it through.' She heard the words out loud and they made her heart hammer inside her, but she was sure she believed them. This was the thing she wanted to say.

'Does that mean you'll help me?' he said.

'If I can.'

He moved to put his hand on her knee but she slid away a little. She didn't want him to think this was easy for her. She didn't want him to think that nothing he'd told her in Turkey was important. 'We have to see this through, Jed,' she clarified. 'I'm here because we can't change the past, but we can change the future.'

He nodded sheepishly. And he bit the edge of his lip like he didn't trust himself not to say something that would spoil things. As he did, a second petal came free from the rose and blew away. 'Thank you,' he said. 'I know I should say other stuff and I know that I don't deserve you to help me and I know—'

She put her hand on his. He stopped talking and nodded. 'So what do you think we should do now?' he said.

She wondered what he meant for a moment. Then

she realised he was talking about right now. About what they should do as the calendar year died. And the reminder that he had barely two months left to find answers made her shiver.

Jed took off his coat and wrapped it around her shoulders. 'What do you think we should do now?' he asked again.

'Well, not stay here all night,' she said through chattering teeth. 'You coming back to mine's a dangerous idea, and I don't think we'd be safe at Nat's place, either.' She pulled the edge of the coat tighter underneath her chin. 'We can't do anything that lets anyone from NOAH know you're back on home ground,' she added.

'So? D'you have any ideas?'

She thought about it carefully. Then she slid the borrowed coat from her shoulders and handed it back to him, stood up and held out her hand to help him up. 'One,' she said.

He looked confused.

'I've got one idea,' she clarified. 'But if it's going to work we have to be quick.'

'Are you sure about this?' Jed tried not to make his voice sound too sceptical, but the leaflet Kassia had given him didn't really seem to be the solution to their problems that she believed it was. At first he'd thought she was offering him money off an all-day breakfast, but then she'd grabbed the leaflet back and made him read the other side. Something about historical buildings doing some kind of heritage thing and keeping their doors open until nearly midnight. A publicity campaign about continuing history across the years. He still had no idea why she wanted him to read it.

'The Monument,' she said, jabbing at the writing.

There seemed to be lots of monuments on the leaflet. That was surely the point of it.

'*The* Monument,' she said again. 'It's really near here and it's open till eleven forty-five.'

'Oh.' He still didn't fully understand. '*The* Monument.'

She grabbed the leaflet and turned towards the entrance of the park. 'It's for *the* Fire of London,' she said as he hurried after her. 'And it's really close. Near St Paul's.'

His footsteps faltered a little.

'We don't have to go to the cathedral,' she said. 'We just have to go somewhere you can hide until we come up with a proper plan.'

He tried to shake the idea of the cathedral from his mind. Its three hundred and sixty-five foot dome acted like a ticking clock, counting down the days until his own year had ended. But the thought felt like the burns on his chest. Impossible to ignore.

He had no time to deal with this, though, because Kassia was already at the gates of the park. 'Come on,' she said. 'We don't have long.' And then she turned away as if she knew those words might hurt him.

The street was strangely quiet. Jed had expected crowds but there was hardly anyone about. One middle-aged lady was dragging a rather reluctant poodle backwards and forwards across a small patch of grass on the kerb-side in an obvious attempt to get the dog to go to the toilet before bedtime. Two teenage boys were having a row. That was it.

'Most people will be down by the river,' Kassia called as she ran. 'Ready for the fireworks. If you're not there early, then you don't get a good spot.'

Jed wondered if Kassia was talking from experience. He doubted Kassia's mum was the sort of person who allowed time off from study to wait on the side of the Thames in December for firework displays. But, then, wasn't it Anna who'd persuaded Kassia that he needed another chance? He could hardly keep up with the thoughts that bashed around inside his head. And he could hardly keep up with Kassia as she raced ahead of him.

49

Jed pulled his watch from his pocket. There were twenty minutes to midnight. Barely moments remaining before one year became another, but somehow the end of the calendar year didn't seem that important. It was the other measure of a year that mattered to him. Midnight before the last day in February was the deadline he was working to. And the weight of that caused him to stumble.

Kassia looked over her shoulder, urging him forward. The physical gap between them had widened. But it was the other gap between them that Jed was worried about. The way Kassia had looked at him and the words she'd said made him think that perhaps things would really be OK. The burns on his chest twinged but he didn't stop running.

'Come on,' she said. She held out her hand and he grabbed hold of it and they ran together.

They turned left on to Gresham Street and raced down Lothbury, Kassia steering them right at the end on to Princes Street. By the time they reached King William Street the burning in Jed's chest had been added to by a stitch in his side.

A street vendor was wheeling a cart towards the river. He wasn't really open for business but Kassia persuaded him to sell them a jumbo bag of crisps, some bottles of water and an enormous bar of chocolate.

'Really?' said Jed, taking the plastic bag from her as she dug around in her pocket for change to pay the vendor.

'You'll need provisions,' she hissed. 'It will take me a while to sort things and this is to keep you going.'

Jed did not like the sound of that. He didn't like to tell her that he wasn't too keen on prawn cocktail flavoured crisps either. He carried the bag as they hurried onwards.

They had to double back on themselves when they reached a line of metal railings that interlocked across the street, obviously there to channel the crowds away from the river once the fireworks were over. Two community officers shouted something, but Jed was running so quickly he couldn't hear it above the sound of his footsteps on the pavement and the air rasping in his lungs.

Suddenly Kassia stopped running. 'There,' she said, pointing at a tall pillar that strained up towards the dark. It reached above all the six or seven storey buildings that ringed around it.

There was a stone cube base at the foot of the pillar, and at the top, lit by floodlights so it shone brightly as if it was day, was something that looked like a large golden ball covered in twisted golden spokes.

'That's it?' he said.

Kassia nodded. 'See the fireball on top?'

So that made sense of the gold. 'But why's it so tall?'

'Something about how if you laid the thing down it would stretch to the place the fire started.'

'And you think this is a good place to hide?' he groaned. 'You don't think a hotel or a hostel or . . .'

'We need somewhere no one from NOAH's going to think of looking. Remember how long we were able to hide out under Paris? This is the same.'

'It is so not the same! It's a concrete pillar! Not a network of tunnels with hidden rooms and caverns.'

'You can go inside,' she said, pointing towards a tiny door in the cube shaped building at the base.

Jed couldn't imagine what could be beyond the door. It was surely just a pillar.

'And no one will think to look here. And you'll be safe until at least January 2nd because tomorrow is a bank holiday and so the Monument will be closed.'

She was planning to leave him here for hours, then. Jed liked the plan less and less.

'Have you got a better idea?' Kassia snapped.

He had no ideas at all. Kassia pulled him forward so they were nearly at the base.

A guard was standing at the entrance. A stream of people was walking past him, stepping out of the

Monument, thanking him as they passed. 'Don't forget,' he called after the visitors, 'Heritage events all across the city marking the New Year.'

Kassia pulled Jed closer. 'I'll distract him,' she said, 'and you get inside.'

'You're not coming in too?' Jed blurted.

'I can't,' said Kassia, pointing to the guard. 'I think that's the last tour group till the day after tomorrow. I have to keep him talking so you can get past.'

'And then what?' Jed knew he sounded frantic, but this really didn't seem the best thought-out plan they'd ever come up with.

'You stay here during the night and I'll be back the day after tomorrow when it reopens.'

'Really?'

'I promise,' she said. 'First thing on January 2nd I'll be back. It will give me time to sort out something proper.'

He guessed his face made it clear how little he was in love with this idea. And also a little of the fear he felt about whether she would actually come back. Surely staying in Postman's Park would have been better than this. As if she could read his mind, Kassia blurted an answer. 'You can't be on the streets when there are so many police about,' she said. 'At just after one, when the crowds leave the river, there'll be police swarming everywhere. I bet NOAH will have an alert out for you so you have to be hidden.'

'Don't you think NOAH believe we died in that balloon crash?' he hissed.

She glared at him. 'Jed. They believe you can live for ever! They might think Dante and me are toast, but they won't stop looking for you until they find you! We can't take any risks!'

Jed wasn't sure that spending a night in a national monument was the answer, but midnight was getting closer. The guard was getting tetchy. He was obviously hoping to get down to the river himself as soon as he could, so every second counted. Jed had to hide somewhere.

Kassia tapped his arm and strode confidently towards the guard.

'What are you doing?' Jed hissed.

'I'm getting you in,' she said. 'Just remember Prague.'

Now she'd really lost her mind. What did she mean about Prague?

'I promise I'll be back,' she added.

Would she really?

'Do you trust me?' she said.

He nodded. More than he trusted himself. He darted out of sight and listened as Kassia began pleading with the guard.

'It was for my birthday,' she yelped, as the guard scowled and made lots of huffing and puffing noises as he fiddled with a ring of keys. 'I left it when I came on the last tour and I really need it back before—' The guard wasn't happy. He rattled his keys, though Jed could see Kassia had managed to get him to step down the front step and slightly away from the door. 'If I don't get it my mum's going to be so mad and I think she'll make a complaint to the council and—'

Jed didn't wait to hear any more. The guard had his back to the door. There were three metres or more between him and the opening. Jed took his chance, turning just enough to catch Kassia's gaze. He nodded then darted inside.

The door closed behind him and he heard a key turn in the lock.

He fumbled his hand along the cold stone wall, found a switch and flicked it on.

A cone of light spilled over him and above him a twisting staircase circled upwards. He took a moment to catch his breath. The floor space was tiny. He began to climb.

The treads spiralled round and round and for a moment Jed wondered if it was best to stop midway and rest. But he didn't. He counted every step he took from the front door and on the stairs. Over three hundred. The number felt strange and familiar. He suddenly realised why. It was over three hundred days since the river. And he knew that just like in the Monument, there wasn't much of a climb left to take.

At the last step, a door jutted into the curve of the wall. Jed tried the handle. It was unlocked and so he pushed the door open and stepped outside. There was a viewing platform netted over with wire which ran all around the stone pillar. Above the platform, the ball of fire jutted out into the night.

Jed rested his weight on the edge of the wire netting just as bells sounded and the sky exploded into light.

Below him, he could see London celebrating as the sky kaleidoscoped with colour. He could almost feel the excitement wafting up to him from the masses that clogged the edge of the river. His own emotions caught inside his aching chest and he slumped to the floor. The fireball blazed above him and the sky shattered and reformed over and over as he watched until he couldn't bear to watch any more. And so he closed his eyes.

He wore the idea that Kassia had been prepared to help him as a coat against the cold, and yet Jed felt an overwhelming sense of loneliness. Here, in the middle of London, as the crowds sang and danced by the side of the river, he was alone under a golden ball of flame. As the people celebrated the birth of a new year, all he could think about was the death of the old. And it was only the belief that Kassia would come back for him that gave him hope.

DAY 308

1st January

'Seriously,' protested Carter, pushing his hand through the arm of his leather coat as he hurried down the corridor. 'Montgomery wants a meeting *now*? The year's only seven hours old. What's the matter with the man?'

Victor tripped on the end of his untied shoe lace. 'I don't think Montgomery does celebrations,' he said, lurching to keep up.

It seemed, though, when they reached the boardroom, that Victor might have been mistaken.

Montgomery stood behind the desk, flanked by Martha Quinn. Both of them were beaming.

Montgomery banged a piece of paper down in front of him.

Carter peered at it. 'We supposed to know what this is?' he said, chomping on a ball of chewing gum.

60

'Survey of the desert in Cappadocia,' explained Martha.

'The site of the balloon crash?' asked Victor.

Montgomery nodded, folded his arms and leant back, clearly expecting a response. Carter and Victor scanned the document, flicking through to the back pages.

'There's nothing there?' said Victor, anxious that this wasn't the answer Montgomery was looking for.

Montgomery beamed even more. 'Exactly! Absolutely nothing. No human remains at all.'

This seemed a rather creepy thing to be extremely excited about. But Montgomery picked up his walking cane and began to pace before Victor could dwell on that thought for too long. 'We expected the unicorn to escape, of course. But the girl and the boy surviving is actually a bonus.'

Victor was confused. Montgomery hadn't intended to kill all those people in the balloon? This was a relief. But he definitely wanted to catch them, and if everyone had got away, why was the guy so happy?

'It means,' cut in Martha Quinn, 'that our targets are still on the run.'

'They could be anywhere again?' said Carter.

'True,' said Montgomery. 'But look.' He gestured towards a huge plasma screen attached to the far wall.

'London transport CCTV cameras. Installed for the protection of customers and drivers. And fitted now, thanks to our initiative, with facial recognition programmes.'

'The same ones as we used in Turkey?' asked Victor, as the screen flickered into life.

'Exactly.'

The grainy footage showed a series of men, women and children clambering on and off a London bus. Then the image froze. A girl with flowers. A boy behind. Martha fiddled with a control panel to make the image sharper and Montgomery clapped his hands.

'They won't be so stupid as to have returned to the flat in Fleet Street,' said Montgomery. 'But we have the proof we need now. The girl and the boy are in London and so I'm pretty sure we can guarantee that the unicorn won't be far behind.'

The other three congratulated themselves loudly. But Victor said nothing. What he felt fizzing inside him, should have been excitement. But he wasn't sure it was.

Kassia sat in the armchair, nibbling the edge of a digestive biscuit. She hadn't wanted to eat anything at all, but her mum had insisted she try. Leaving Jed safe in the Monument for so long had seemed like the only option while they came up with a plan. But Kassia couldn't help thinking about how alone he must feel. Worry made the biscuit taste like cardboard.

Dante thumped the coffee table beside her. It was his not so subtle way of getting her attention and making it clear that he wanted to talk. 'You OK?' he signed quickly.

Kassia shrugged. She had no idea how to answer that. It felt odd being in her uncle's front room again. The last time she'd seen this room, it had been through a computer screen. She'd been in Paris and had finally Skyped her uncle to ask for advice about how to make Jed better. Then, things had been desperate. And it all felt pretty desperate now. And yet again her uncle seemed the best person to ask for help.

At Christmas, Kassia had caught him up to speed with what had happened in the months they'd been away. Now Nat had new information to deal with. Jed was back in London. So they needed a plan.

The door of her uncle's study swung open. Nat was still wearing his hospital scrubs and a conical hat with the words 'Happy New Year' in bright red letters around the rim. 'OK,' he said with his voice and his fingers, making sure that Dante could follow the conversation. 'I think we have it all set up.'

'You're sure he'll be safe?' Kassia asked. Being in London, so close to NOAH's headquarters in The Shard, terrified her. All the tracking NOAH had done abroad made it clear that if Jed was in close range there'd be very little that could stop the organisation from pressing in.

'I don't think we can make any guarantees,' said Nat, straightening his hat. 'But he'll be safer than staying here or at yours.'

Kassia tried to swallow the last chunk of biscuit, but it wedged in her throat.

'I think the best thing we can hope,' Nat went on rather loudly, 'is that NOAH haven't noticed you're back, and that the two of you go off the radar again with Jed just as soon as possible.'

'Now hold on!' Anna had been standing patiently by the window and this response from her brother made her pitch towards the centre of the room. 'You can't leave again!'

'But I have to,' stuttered Kassia. 'We both have to. Now Jed's here, the three of us are too obvious a target in Fleet Street.' Surely she didn't have to remind her mum that NOAH knew exactly where they lived. It had taken over six months to rebuild the flat after NOAH's last little visit.

Anna leant forward, reaching to brush away the

biscuit crumbs on Kassia's blouse, then stopped herself. 'I know,' she whispered.

Kassia took her mum's hand and held it for a moment. She could see that her mum was trying to find the right thing to say.

'So where have you found for us?' asked Dante.

Nat adjusted his hat again, and then, as if only now aware that it was probably making him look silly, he took it off. 'It's not really a where. It's a who,' he said. 'Charlie Monalees.'

'I know that name,' said Kassia.

'He's American,' went on Nat. 'Worked in Heidelberg.'

Kassia was swamped with memories. 'Oh, yes,' she said. 'He helped us escape from the hospital after we had to jump in the river and . . .' She lifted her hand instinctively to the faded scorch marks at the base of her neck. The thought of how they'd had to use a machine to restart her heart still unnerved her. 'He saved my life,' she added quietly.

'Yep, well, he's prepared to save your life again,' said Nat.

'You want us to go back to Germany?' Dante asked. 'Seriously? Because we've done the whole German thing and it really didn't end well.'

'Charlie's in London,' cut in Nat. 'He lost his job

as a paramedic in Heidelberg.'

'It wasn't because of faking our death certificates, was it?' Kassia said.

'All he said was it was time to try somewhere new,' Nat mumbled, and the way he spoke made Kassia think that her uncle was a little jealous that someone had been able to get away from their place of work, whatever their reason for leaving. Kassia wondered if Nat was still making mistakes at the hospital or if things had settled down for him. She was suddenly ashamed that she knew nothing about what her uncle had been up to since they'd been away. She and Dante had just crashed back into his life and were demanding help again.

There wasn't time to ask about anything else now, though, and her uncle continued talking. 'Charlie transferred to London rather than going back to Chicago where he's from. Once he was in the city, it didn't take much to work out that I was the doctor who first dealt with Jed when he clambered out of the Thames.' This made sense. The story had been all over the international news as well as the local press. A boy appearing from the water, remembering nothing and recognised by no one, tended to make headline news whatever country you were in. 'Anyway, Charlie and I got chatting and it became clear that he's a good guy to call on in times of trouble. So I rang him just now.'

'And he's going to let the three of us stay at his house?' asked Dante.

Nat twanged the elastic chin-strap of the discarded party hat with his fingers. 'Not exactly.'

Kassia looked at her uncle.

'Charlie doesn't have a house. He actually lives . . . somewhere else.'

Kassia looked over anxiously at her mum.

'Trust me,' Nat pressed on again brightly, 'Charlie's going to help. And the plan he has is perfect.'

DAY 309

2nd January

Jed watched the sun rise across the Thames, the light seeping across the expanse of Tower Bridge. He pulled his coat tighter round his chest and tried to stop shivering. He wasn't sure that he had ever been so cold.

He had slept the night in the opening at the top of the stairs so that he could shelter from the worst of the wind, but he'd been scared to sleep at the bottom of the stairs where it was warmer, just in case a guard came back to check on things. He'd spent most of January 1st pacing up and down the stairwell just to make sure he kept moving. He'd read a copy of the guidebook that he'd taken from the payment desk and he'd rationed the provisions, even downing a handful of prawn cocktail crisps on the hour every hour.

Now, though, it was January 2nd. Kassia had promised she'd come back today. Any minute, the Monument would reopen and a tour group was bound to appear. That was why he was outside on the viewing platform. Waiting.

He and Kassia hadn't really talked about what would happen. But twenty-four hours of being alone had helped Jed come up with a plan. He'd hide behind the door to the viewing platform and then merge with the tour group when they arrived. He could only hope that no one compared the numbers of visitors in and out of the building.

Suddenly, there was a noise at the bottom of the stairs. The main door was opening. He could hear whistling. The guard, perhaps. And voices bouncing up the stairwell, distorted and sounding too loud.

He pulled the door to the platform back hard against himself. His blood was surging in his ears and his fingers shook as he held the door steady.

There were voices on the stairs now.

Footsteps getting closer.

Heavy breathing. Gasps for air as feet pounded each of the curling steps.

And then there were people on the platform, cameras raised, elbows jostling against each other for the best positions to see the view.

Jed took a deep breath. Then he slipped out from behind the door and out into the open.

And a hand came from behind him and clamped firmly over his mouth.

Jed struggled to twist free. He turned and pulled. But the hand pressed tighter. He could hardly breathe. He drove his foot down hard trying to connect with the foot of whoever was holding him. The hand across his face juddered for a moment, the owner of the vice like grip reacting to the pain.

Jed tried to escape, but whoever was pressing their palm across his mouth was using his other hand to hold his arms.

Jed dug deep and jerked his shoulders one final, frantic time. He staggered forward and turned to face whoever it was who'd held him.

Dante.

Jed groaned.

Dante shrugged. Then bent down to rub his foot.

'It's been a while,' signed Dante, standing up straight again.

Jed could only shake his head in answer.

'How many times do you want me to say sorry?' Dante's signing was getting wilder with each repetition of the apology. 'I wanted to smuggle you down

70

without other people noticing. I didn't want you to make a scene.'

'That was to *stop* there being a scene?' Jed objected, failing to turn his response into sign language. 'Brilliant plan!' Jed couldn't help wondering if the harsh treatment was connected to Kassia sharing the truth about why they'd left Turkey. Dante was nothing if not a protective brother.

'I should have come up for you,' said Kassia, who was between them.

'You think?' groaned Jed.

'I was with the guard making sure he didn't notice you coming out again,' she said defensively.

To be fair, though, part of the plan had worked well. As far as the guard was concerned there had been absolutely no overnight visitors in the Monument. Jed had to admit that it hadn't been too terrible a place to hide. And now that Kassia was here he felt a hundred times better than when he'd been working his way through the prawn cocktail crisps. Still, he could have done without Dante's efforts to keep him quiet. However good the hiding place, the thought of NOAH catching up with him was never far away.

And so with that in mind, Jed had been keen to see what Kassia had come up with.

The hope was wearing a little thin as the three of

them hurried along the towpath by Regent's Canal, weighed down with Kassia and Dante's bags of clothes and provisions. 'When you said Venice, I thought you meant Italy,' he mumbled.

'No,' said Kassia. 'The emphasis was on the word *Little*.'

Jed wasn't sure he'd ever heard of a place called Little Venice. Two bus rides later, and a quick walk down Bloomfield Road, he had a better idea about what it was.

The Regent's and the Grand Canal cut across a part of London that was lined with incredibly expensive looking houses. Most of them had fancy mailboxes and huge electric gates attached to outside pillars, so it was hard to tell what the houses actually looked like, but they were definitely posh.

'Nice,' said Jed, as they hurried past a particularly large panelled fence guarded by two concrete lions.

'It will make a change from hiding in sewers or caves,' signed Dante.

'There's still no guarantee that we'll be safe from NOAH,' warned Kassia. 'We need to be careful and watch everything we do.'

Jed reasoned that behind one of these large electric gates it would be pretty easy to be careful about security and he was keen to see exactly which house

Kassia's uncle had in mind for them.

But Kassia had stopped walking. 'Here,' she said, glancing at a small piece of paper, checking the address.

Jed looked back towards the concrete lions. 'Here?' he said hopefully.

'Yes,' said Kassia. She turned away from the road and waved her hand towards a long narrowboat that was moored by the side of the canal.

Jed felt a wave of discomfort.

The boat had a long black base, and its sides were painted pillarbox red. Square windows were edged with cream, and at one end a small round window looked out on the canal bank. The roof was crowded with pot plants and there was an open section at the front of the boat where a canvas cover had been poppered into place to protect against the January weather.

There was the sound of a zip sliding open. The side of fabric swung free and a tall man, in a striped top and with a pencil behind his ear, pushed his head out of the opening.

'Charlie?' exclaimed Jed. 'From the hospital in Heidelberg?'

The young man grinned and beckoned them towards the opening, taking their bags. 'Best you don't go mentioning Heidelberg,' he laughed. 'What happened in Germany stays in Germany. Understand?'

Jed nodded and reached out his hand to help Kassia step into the opening on the boat. He thought for a moment about helping Dante aboard too, but Dante made the jump for himself.

Charlie glanced quickly along the canal bank and then re-zipped the fabric into position and ushered them down the steps into the main part of the boat. The inside was panelled with wood. Comfy settees lined each wall and there was a galley kitchen and what Jed assumed must be bedrooms beyond the living area. He nodded appreciatively. The house with the lion statues melted away. This was nice.

'So,' said Charlie brightly. 'Welcome aboard. You're welcome to stay here as long as you like, of course. But I guess you have a plan.'

Jed's warm feeling evaporated.

'Thank you,' he said quietly. He said nothing about the fact that as far as he knew, the three of them had absolutely no plan at all.

DAY 310

3rd January

Victor had been offered a chair, but he wasn't keen to sit down. There was too much nervous energy surging through his body. He paced backwards and forwards in front of the small lead-lighted window of the Reverend's office in St Paul's Cathedral.

Reverend Cockren watched him from his seat behind the desk.

'Why the change of strategy?' Victor demanded. 'You've spent weeks shutting me out and suddenly you send a letter saying you want to chat, then keep me waiting for days until I can see you.'

'Perhaps I believed you when you said we were running out of time,' said the Reverend.

This was an odd answer. Victor couldn't see the logic of the statement, but if they were talking about time then he was absolutely certain they had none of it available to be playing mind games with. 'Do you remember my father?' he said.

The Reverend picked up a pen from the desk and twisted it between his fingers. 'Not really,' he said, looking intently at the pen, as if he expected it to do something incredible like burst into flames. 'Your father was away a lot. Working. Trying to find answers.' The pen stilled. 'My own father was interested in answers. And he worked hard.'

'Really?' Victor had no idea where this was going or what the Reverend's dad had to do with things.

'My father joined an organisation.'

'What, like NOAH?' pressed Victor. Surely that could be the only reason to bring the old man into the conversation.

The Reverend laughed mockingly at this suggestion. 'It was a brotherhood. One concerned with the work of an alchemist.'

Victor turned away from the window. 'Are we talking about Fulcanelli?'

Reverend Cockren didn't answer. It was as if he had prepared a speech and was determined to deliver it without swerving from the script. 'My father was a good man but he was driven by a desire for – ' he hesitated as if the next word had lodged somewhere in his throat – 'money,' he said at last. He twisted the pen again and Victor saw the tiniest drop of ink bleed on to his thumb. 'But money failed to make my father happy. And I think there was something about the work of the brotherhood he didn't understand.'

Victor was confused. If the brotherhood worked for Fulcanelli then they knew about the elixir. That it made him live for ever. His ability to survive drowning in the River Neckar and an explosion in a car had made that perfectly clear. What was there not to understand?

But Reverend Cockren had more to say. 'Years after my father started his work, I began to think about the brotherhood's work on eternal life. And I wondered whether perhaps life should be measured in other ways, apart from its length.'

Victor stopped his pacing. This was ridiculous. He'd come here for answers about his own dad and this man was just rambling on. 'Why are you telling me this?' he protested. 'You think the work NOAH is doing to achieve Absolute Health is wrong? How can it not be good to want to live for ever?'

Reverend Cockren gripped the pen tightly between his ink-stained fingers. 'I'm trying to tell you that the value of a person's life is something that isn't measured in days.' He seemed uncertain for a moment about whether he should say more. 'I'm trying to tell you that this is a secret your father came to understand before he died.'

What was the man going on about? Victor stepped away from the window and drove his hands down on to the desk. He stared the chaplain right in the eyes and Reverend Cockren did not look away. 'My father was trying to capture Fulcanelli. He wanted the world to know the secret of the elixir.'

The Reverend didn't shift his gaze and his eyes burned blue. 'Maybe the secret that actually needs sharing is the one your father and his friend, Tristan Devaux, wanted to share with Fulcanelli.'

It had been nearly a week since they'd arrived in Little Venice and taken refuge in Charlie's narrowboat. *The Voyager* was certainly comfortable, although it didn't do much voyaging. In fact, it hadn't left the dock since the three of them had arrived. Charlie had offered to take them to any place the canal network made possible, but it was hard to voyage anywhere if you had no idea where you were going.

'You three come up with a sensible plan yet?' Charlie asked, licking sweet and sour sauce from his fingers, then clearing a space for his plate at the end of the table, which was now laden with tubs of takeaway. It was the first evening meal with them that his shift work at the hospital had allowed and he was obviously keen to feel involved.

Kassia held out her plate for Dante to give her some

rice. She guessed her silence was a good enough answer.

'Explain it to me,' pressed Charlie. 'Are you after finding the recipe to make the elixir? Or the actual elixir itself?'

Jed raised his eyebrows and Kassia turned the question into sign for Dante. The words sounded ridiculous when said aloud and even more crazy somehow when turned into sign language.

'We thought we were looking for the recipe at first,' Jed said, signing the answer himself to save Kassia a job. 'But after Turkey and the memories, I think there *is* a sixth bottle somewhere.'

Charlie's eyes widened in excitement.

'I think,' Jed continued, 'that the Brothers of Heliopolis swore to protect the bottles. There were special Keepers of the Elixir.' He waited uncertainly for a moment until Kassia nodded for him to go on. She knew now that her dad had been a Keeper. But this didn't mean the story shouldn't be told.

'We think the sixth bottle is still hidden,' Jed said.

'This bottle could be anywhere, though, right?' pressed Charlie.

Dante watched Kassia translate the question before answering. 'There have always been *signs*,' he signed jokingly. 'Connected signs, that worked like clues. Like we were on this massive treasure hunt.'

'But you have no idea where the treasure is yet?' said Charlie.

Kassia shook her head.

Charlie was undeterred. 'So where do the signs lead now, then?'

Kassia put down her fork, grabbed a notebook and pressed it beside her plate of rice and beef chow mein. 'Well, after we left you in Heidelberg and did the whole death wagon thing, there were the story stones in Prague,' she said. 'And then in Turkey, there were the coloured stages of alchemy.'

'So you're looking for more signs sort of "out in the world"?'

Jed sighed loudly.

'It's what we *should* be doing,' ventured Kassia. 'But to be honest, we don't know where to look.'

'We spent weeks in Paris hunting through books on alchemy,' cut in Jed, 'trying to find ideas about where signs could be hidden.'

'And?' Charlie was obviously finding it hard to hide his exasperation.

'And nothing,' snapped Jed. He pushed his plate away. 'The Keepers of the Elixir were guarding a secret. So the *secret* part is still a big deal.'

'Don't you just have to get out there, looking for symbols, like you did in Prague?' Charlie said nervously. 'I'm just saying. It might be a start.'

'NOAH are watching,' said Kassia. 'In a city like London, there will be eyes everywhere.'

'So you have to be careful and clever,' said Charlie. 'Don't go out together. Vary the times you leave this place so there's no pattern.'

'What we have to be is quick,' said Jed, making eye contact with nobody.

Charlie looked confused.

'There's a time limit,' said Kassia, her gaze, too, fixed on some distant point beyond them.

'How long have you got?'

'Till the last day in February,' said Jed.

Kassia flicked through the calendar in her head. Not in months. Time was measured now in smaller fragments.

'That's seven weeks away.'

Kassia noticed that everyone had stopped eating.

DAY 322
15th January

Jed sat in the half-light of the lounge area in the narrowboat. He held a piece of paper in his hand. A countdown chart. The paper was weathered from continual folding. He wanted to wait until midnight until he crossed out another date. No, what he *really* wanted to do was to stop time and make it unnecessary to make another mark on the tattered paper he'd carried around half the world with him.

How had this happened? How had months become weeks? Just over six of them?

He remembered how once he and Kassia had sat on a kerbside in Prague, talking about how long they had left to find the elixir. It had been nine months then. The time needed for a human baby to begin and grow and be born.

That conversation had been a lifetime ago.

◀

NUMENT
DON EYE
CATHEDRAL
F LONDON

NTIL 11.45
BER 31ST

LONDON

40)
04/03 17.05.34

THE GREAT
OF LONDO

The Great Fire of London was a
major conflagration that swept
through the central parts of the
English city of London from
Sunday, 2 September to
Wednesday, 5 September 1666.
The fire gutted the medieval City
of London inside the old Roman
city wall. It threatened but did
not reach the aristocratic district
of Westminster, Charles II's
Palace of Whitehall, and most of
the suburban slums. It consumed
13,200 houses, 87 parish
churches, St Paul'

City authorit
to have destro
70,000 of th
inhabitants.

The death toll
traditionally th
been small, as
deaths were
reasoning has
challenged on th
the deaths o
middle-class pec
recorded whil

What could be made in only six weeks?

He sighed and looked up as shadow flicked across the line of light.

'Hey,' Dante nodded at him. 'What's that?'

Jed hastily re-creased the folds. 'Nothing.'

Dante shrugged, leant down and took the paper from Jed's hand.

Jed saw the colour drain a little from Dante's face, but he couldn't be sure it wasn't the effect of the flicker of the lamp.

Dante passed the paper back. 'It's not nothing,' he signed. 'It's *everything* really, isn't it?'

Jed bit his lip and stuffed the paper back into his pocket. 'Kassia doesn't like to see me counting down.'

Dante sank into the seat opposite.

'This is such a mess,' Jed went on. 'We've got no one to help us. No trails to follow.'

'But we're looking,' signed Dante. 'We've been out every day this week trying to find clues.' He pointed to the stack of photos on the table down the other end of the boat. 'At least we have a sort of system now.'

'Great,' groaned Jed. 'Lion sculptures; statues of Eros; angels from the city of London. A whole river of ink and I feel like I'm drowning.' He plunged his hands through his hair, before fumbling for signs to continue. 'So much and so little,' he said at last. 'How are we supposed to know what any of it means? If any of it is important? Whether it's all just a waste of time?'

Dante frowned. 'Are you saying that all our efforts . . .' His signs stalled a little but he shook his head and carried on. 'That everything any of us from this family has done is wasted?'

Jed took a moment before he realised what Dante was talking about. 'Your dad?' he signed slowly.

'We don't need to go there,' Dante signed quickly.

'No. I should explain.'

'Kassia did.'

Jed tried to keep his breathing steady.

'I'm still angry,' Dante signed. 'Even though I know it wasn't your fault. It's just that you were there. And now he's gone. You know? The anger sort of sneaks up every so often.'

'I kind of thought that from the welcome you gave me at the top of the Monument.'

Dante shrugged. 'I'm trying to deal with it. I guess you can *see* what I think.' He froze his final sign by way of explanation. 'Kassia's trying to deal too. But maybe her thoughts are more hidden.'

Jed bit his lip again. He wanted to look away but he needed to keep focusing on Dante's hands.

'Kind of funny, don't you think, that it was our mum who ended up defending you?'

'I suppose people change,' signed Jed and suddenly his hands tightened as if this word was the wrong one to use. He made the sign again slowly. *Change*. It felt awkward on his fingers. He stood up and peered out of the window.

A single street lamp on the towpath lit the space beyond the boat as he stared across the canal.

Dante stood too and moved beside him, his hands raised in sign. 'What are you thinking, Jed?'

The answers tumbled from Jed's fingers. 'That I don't know what to do. That change is important. And that if this was a river there would be waves and the boat would be moving and we would be flowing somewhere; moving in some direction even if it wasn't the right one. But we're on this man-made canal, going nowhere! And I don't know what to do!'

'So we keep looking,' Dante signed boldly. 'We keep collecting those signs and we keep trying to find clues.'

Jed didn't reply. He couldn't explain to Dante what he was really beginning to think. He wasn't sure of it himself.

DAY 326
19th January

The gravestone was unassuming. There were no carved angels, no crosses, no anchors.

The grass was patchy, greener in places than the grass that surrounded the plot. This was because the turf was younger, more recently planted.

Jed had spent the morning pounding the streets of the city. They had broken the day into shifts, as they did every day now. He was due back to the narrowboat in less than half an hour. He knew Dante would be sorting through the photos and images they had collected the day before. And he was scared that, like the hours they'd spent reading the alchemy books in Paris, these searches would lead nowhere.

The Brothers of Heliopolis were formed to keep secrets. They had known what they were doing when they hid the elixir. Because they had known what would happen if the elixir fell into the wrong hands.

That's why he was here.

Jed bent down and ran his finger across the newly-carved name on the gravestone: JACOB ZANE.

For a second Jed's fingers burnt, just as they had when Jacob had hung on to them as he'd dangled over the edge of the tower of Notre Dame Cathedral.

If Jacob hadn't been so desperate for the elixir for himself, and so sure that having the secret to eternal life would lead him to power and glory, Jed would have had the recipe. This whole race against time would have been over.

But Jed didn't feel angry. He felt confused.

The memories of the days he'd taken the elixir woke him sometimes, the guilt about what he had done overwhelming him. But memories of that night on the tower of Notre Dame didn't make him feel guilty. He hadn't let Jacob fall. Jacob had been so desperate for the elixir, he'd given up his life.

Something about this memory made Jed feel pain sharper and deeper than guilt, though.

He plunged his hands into his pocket and folded his fingers over the countdown chart he carried with him. He didn't need to take the paper out to see the number of weeks remaining. And weeks were not the measure that mattered any more. He worked in days. And he knew there were forty.

It reminded him of a story he'd once heard involving forty days.

It was the time Jesus had wandered lost in the wilderness, being tempted by the devil.

DAY 330
23rd January

Jed was sitting at the table and Kassia was standing in the galley. She'd been polishing the inside of a saucepan with a drying-up cloth for what seemed like hours.

The silver pocket watch was on the table. Jed stared down at it. 'Where are Dante and Charlie?' According to their timetable, the symbol-hunting for the day should have been done by now.

'Gone to get food,' said Kassia, her polishing stopping for a second before she began again with even more vigour. 'Do you want a drink?'

Jed leant back so that his head touched the window and laughed weakly. 'Well, yes. A particular drink, if I'm honest.'

Kassia's hand stilled and the cloth fluttered limply free of the confines of the saucepan.

'But if we knew where it was or how to make it,

you wouldn't be trying to bore a hole in the bottom of a pan with nothing more than a duster and I wouldn't be staring at hands ticking round a silver watchface.'

Kassia blew out a breath. She put the saucepan down on the work surface and hung up the cloth. Then she sat beside Jed and picked up the pocket watch, snapping it closed so that the face was no longer visible. The engraved swallow in flight looked up at her. 'We've come a long way since you made me a sugar bird, haven't we?'

Jed leant forward again, his elbows on the table and his chin resting in his hands. 'Yep. So far. And yet it feels like we're back at the beginning.'

Kassia closed her hand across the watch so that even the engraved swallow was out of sight. 'Do you want to talk about what happened in Turkey?' she asked quietly. 'Inside the Dark Church?'

Jed's forehead wrinkled in confusion. Had she been talking to Dante again about what happened with her dad? Was she still angry, like Dante had admitted he was? Was she hiding what she really felt? 'You want me to remind you about how I hurt you and about all the things I did in the past?' he asked nervously. This didn't seem like the greatest plan.

'No. I want you to talk to me about the Emerald

Tablet. About what it means and about where we go from here.'

Jed flopped his hands back down on the table. 'I don't *know* where we go!' How many times could he keep saying this?

'But the Tablet? Maybe we're missing stuff that will help us as we look for clues.'

'I've told you. It talked about things above being as below.'

'And you think *that* was the recipe for the elixir?'

Jed couldn't blame her for sounding desperate. They'd raced across the whole of Turkey, been hurled out of a hot air balloon and risked life and death trials in a city below the ground, all to get the chance to look at a slab of green stone which was supposed to hold answers. 'No,' he said gently. 'It wasn't a recipe.' He tried not to think about Notre Dame and his recent visit to Jacob's grave. 'It was just yet another clue in this messed-up puzzle.'

'And you don't know what it means?' she pressed.

Jed waited before he answered. He could see that Kassia was biting the edge of her lip. 'No. I thought it meant that I had to face my past. I did that.' He could hear the strain in his voice. 'And that turned out brilliantly, as you know.'

Kassia's hand was gripped so tightly around the

pocket watch that her knuckles were white. 'What you said about my dad dying was difficult to hear.'

Jed could only whisper his answer. 'It was difficult to say.'

He looked across the boat to the other window. It was just possible to see the water of the canal, still, like glass. 'I've started to wonder,' Jed went on, 'about all this chasing for answers. All this racing, to make my abnormal lifespan longer.' The words sounded ugly and he looked away from the window and back down at the top of the table. 'Should we be doing it?' he said.

'Of course!' Kassia snapped.

He didn't look at her. 'Why?'

She grabbed his arm with her free hand. 'Because you started something and you are so close to finishing it.'

He struggled to get free. 'What if I shouldn't? What if living for ever is a really bad idea?' He saw Jacob's gravestone clearly inside his mind. It wasn't just how Jacob had wanted the elixir to gain power that troubled him. This was more personal. 'What if I get stuck at this age and the world gets older around me and all I can do is watch?' Kassia still clung to his arm but he drove on with his argument. 'What if you get older and Dante gets older. And everyone who's helped me.'

ABOUT MONUMENT

he Monument to the Great Fire of London, more commonly
own simply as the Monument, is a Doric column in the City
London, near the northern end of London Bridge, that
mmemorates the Great Fire of London.

t stands at the junction of Monument Street and Fish Street
ill, 202 ft (62 m) tall and 202 ft (62 m) from the spot in
dding Lane where the Great Fire started on 2 September
. Another monument, the Golden Boy of Pye Corner, marks
point near Smithfield where the fire was stopped.
onstructed between 1671 and 1677, it was built on the
St. Margaret's, Fish Street, the first church to h
e Great Fire.

To visit The Monument, please visit
www.themonument.info

The Voy

FIREWORK SAF

LIGHT UP THE NIGHT ON NEW

Whether you want to light a sparkler or design an eye-catching display for your town, here are a few tips to be mindful of before starting the show!

Keep it legal. Most injuries sustained as a result of fireworks are from illegal fireworks. How can you tell if yours are illegal? Avoid fireworks packaged in brown paper - these are usually intended for professional displays and not for consumers!

Keep water close. Always keep a bucket of water nearby for emergencies. Make sure to dowse burned fireworks with water before binning them too.

Brought to you by the UK Firework Association in Conjunction with the Mayor of Londo

The words were burning his throat but he knew he had to say out loud all the things he'd been thinking for weeks. 'What if I just stay – ' he pulled his arm free – 'like this for ever? Would you want that? To stay just as you are for all time?'

Kassia's eyes were wide. Her cheeks were flushed. 'What is the alternative?' she stammered. 'We've got just over one month left before the year is up. That's all! So you can't think about what would happen if we don't find the elixir.'

Jed pulled himself up to stand and stumbled towards the worktop. He reached out his arm to steady himself, catching the edge of the saucepan. The pan fell to the floor, the metal chiming against the wooden floor like a bell. 'So I find a way to live for ever, whatever the cost? Is that what you're saying?'

She put the pocket watch back on the table, flicking the case open so that the face was visible again. The hands ticked onwards. 'Yes. That's exactly what I'm saying,' she said.

DAY 332

25th January

Victor snapped off the television and stumbled towards the sound of the knocking. He picked up a bar of chocolate from the table and fumbled for the lock.

The guard on the other side of the door looked at him hopefully.

'What about your diet?' Victor quizzed.

'Oh, come on, mate,' the guard said. 'What I eat at work, my wife doesn't need to know about.'

Victor grinned and handed over the chocolate. 'What have you got for me?'

The guard held out a small flat package. 'Feels like some sort of book.'

Victor nodded. He took the parcel and ran his finger along the external postmark. 'Thanks,' he said.

Victor liked books. If the story was a good one.

DAY 339

1st February

Kassia stumbled over the entrance into the narrowboat and hurried to the galley kitchen. She put a large cardboard box on the table, blew out cold air that rose in a cloud like breath from a dragon, and then clapped her hands together in a desperate attempt to warm them.

'What's that?' signed Dante from his position beside the sink, his fingers dripping soap suds on to the floor.

Kassia took a moment to answer. She didn't want them to be cross with her.

'Kass? The box? What is it?' Dante's signs were more deliberate and the soap suds sprayed even further.

Kassia looked at Jed, who was sifting through a pile of photos and maps of London. She could tell from the way his eyes narrowed that Jed knew exactly what the box was.

'OK, don't get mad. I arranged to meet Mum and she brought it.'

Dante moved forward to argue, but Kassia cut him off before he could let his hands speak.

'Don't panic. I used the coded email system like we used from Paris, and I didn't meet her at home and I was really careful.'

'What is it?' Dante's hands blurted.

Kassia glanced at Jed again.

'It's the box I found months ago, isn't it?' he replied slowly. 'The things from your childhood. Stuff from with your dad.'

Kassia nodded. She lifted the lid. A plasticine tortoise grinned up at her from on top of a pile of notebooks and paintings. 'I thought that, as Dad was a Keeper of the Elixir, there might be a clue here. I know it's a long shot. It's all we have of him without going back to the farmhouse in Spain. But I wondered if it was worth looking. Just in case.'

Kassia dug her hands into the box. She cleared a space on the table and put the notebooks and childhood paintings in a pile. At the bottom of the box was a small book. A published book this time, not a notebook filled with childhood stories. She passed it to Jed.

'My dad's favourite poems,' she said quietly.

'You think a book of poetry will help us?' asked Dante.

Kassia twisted round to face him so that her signs could be clearly read. 'I *don't* know what will help. I'm clutching at straws like we all are.'

She felt a hand on her arm. 'It was worth a try,' said Jed. He wasn't signing because with one hand he still clutched tightly to the book.

DAY 345
7th February

Victor and Carter had been called to look at the plasma screen again.

'Look,' said Montgomery, gesturing at the image. It was more footage from inside a London bus, this time pulling away from a cemetery, though the focus was less clear. 'You see. It's him. I'm sure of it.'

Victor scrunched his eyes up. He wasn't convinced. It could have been, perhaps. But he kind of felt Montgomery's words were edged with wishful thinking.

'The unicorn is out there!' Montgomery bellowed.

Victor stepped away from the screen and folded his arms across his chest. His boss was clearly rattled.

'And I am losing patience!' Montgomery added, breathing deeply and trying, but failing, to regain his composure.

He reached under the desk and pulled out a small tray of what looked like thick plastic buttons.

'Tracking devices?' asked Carter, pulling a length of gum from between his teeth then snapping it back inside his mouth and chewing vigorously.

Montgomery nodded and gestured for Victor and Carter to take some. 'If you make any contact with the target, you get a fix on him so we do not lose him again,' hissed Montgomery.

Victor took a couple of the tracking buttons and pushed them into his pocket. One caught on the edge of a photograph he kept there and he reached his hand back inside his pocket to straighten it. He smoothed the corners of the photo over and over with his thumb, trying to avoid the feel of the button against his hand as he moved and turned towards the door.

DAY 352

14th February

Kassia lifted the kettle and put it on the hob. The metal base clanged against the grill that fenced the burners. They were there to stop things slipping off the oven if the narrowboat hit rough water. The metal against metal made a sound like a bell. Kassia grimaced. She'd been trying to be quiet. When she'd crept past Jed's bedroom, he'd still been asleep, the book of poems open on his bedcovers. Now she'd definitely woken him.

'I'm so sorry.'

He tousled his hair and swept it back from his face. 'For what?'

She waved her hand in the direction of the hob, causing the kettle to clang against the metal fencing again.

Jed hurried over and steered her towards the seating.

'Let me do that,' he said.

Kassia sat down and watched as the kettle boiled, releasing a cloud of steam. Jed mixed coffee and put two mugs on the table and sat next to her.

'Are you OK?' she said, linking her fingers round the mug and soaking in the warmth.

'Sure,' he laughed. 'I'm going to live for ever.'

Despite the warmth from the mug, Kassia felt cold.

Jed drank quietly, then he put the mug on the table again and leant back on the seating. His head touched the window, his hair squashed against the glass. 'This place is driving me mad,' he complained. 'I need to get out.'

Kassia looked across at the sketchy timetable they'd pinned to the wall. 'You're out first shift this afternoon,' she said, trying to sound encouraging.

He sighed and then banged his hands down on the table. Now it was his turn to say sorry for making noise. 'This isn't about the elixir,' he said through gritted teeth. 'This is about being here. Look,' he said, waving his hand towards the oven. 'Even the kettle's got a cage.' He stood up and linked his hands behind his head, his elbows jutting out into the room and one of them catching on the drawstring for the light. 'See,' he fumed. 'I need . . .'

'What?'

'Just a morning.' He clasped his hands together as if begging her. 'Without a timetable like the ones your mum made you have when you were studying.'

She tried not to show how much his words stung her. 'We have to have a plan!'

'I know!' he groaned. 'But I just want one morning. Like we had in Paris. When we ate cake.'

'You want cake?' she said.

'No!' he groaned, even more loudly this time, before sinking into the seat beside her. 'I want to get out of here and live a little. Together.'

'It's not safe,' she said. 'We agreed. We go out alone. We stick to the rules.'

'But this?' he said, pressing his hands on the table. 'Is this living?'

She could tell her face was showing something close to anger by the way he responded.

'I don't mean being here with you. I just mean being here. Being trapped. Not able to do anything. *Together.*' He repeated the final word loudly for extra emphasis.

'But NOAH?' she reminded him. 'We can't take any risks.'

'What is it all for, then?' he said quietly. 'Supposing we never work out the clues, Kass? Supposing the time ticks on and . . .'

He didn't finish his sentence. She didn't need him to. 'What would we do?' she said.

'Something I promised we'd go back to do. Remember?'

There was only one thing she remembered promising they'd return to do. Surely he couldn't mean *that*. That was madness.

'This *is* madness,' Kassia said, grabbing hold of Jed's hand.

They had argued for about an hour. She had begged him. Pointed out all the reasons they shouldn't. But his mind had been unchangeable. 'I want to live a bit,' he'd said. 'If we can't solve this and I'm going to die, I need to know we did more than just wait for time to pass.'

She had no answer for that.

They'd taken two buses across London to Somerset House. Kassia remembered the promise. It had been on their first walk out of Fleet Street, in the very first weeks after Jed had clambered from the River Thames. Kassia had shown him the courtyard of the enormous building and she'd explained how in winter it housed an ice rink. And they had made a promise to come back.

'So your mum would really hate you doing this?'

Jed said laughingly as he checked Kassia's boot laces for her, pulled her up to stand and then led the way as they stepped cautiously on to the edge of the ice.

Kassia clung tightly to his arm with one hand and to the wall around the rink with the other. 'My mum would have a fit!' she giggled. Then she hesitated. 'Except, I don't know . . . Maybe now she wouldn't. She's changed, you know. While we've been away.'

The blades of their boots cut into the ice.

Kassia lurched nervously, gripping so tightly to the wall and Jed that her knuckles turned white.

'And have you changed?' Jed asked, easing her gently forward and nodding supportively as her feet spluttered, slipping erratically. 'Just trust the ice and try to glide.'

Kassia looked down at the ice, so cold and solid. 'Maybe?' she said, her feet slowing and her arm floundering along the top of the wall. 'I guess I wouldn't have thought I could do this.'

'Ice skate?' Jed laughed, steering her onwards and taking her hands so that he was holding them both and able to ease her away from the safety of the wall. 'Because I hate to disappoint you, but I'm not so totally sure you can.'

She wobbled again. 'Hey!'

He had turned so he was skating backwards,

not able to see where he was going but focused totally on her.

'I'm doing OK,' she said.

'You're doing more than OK,' he said, guiding them closer to the centre of the rink.

Kassia's hands clutched his even more tightly. 'Wait. I need to . . .' Her legs wobbled. She sank further, her knees bending as her feet slid apart.

'Head up,' he encouraged. 'Keep your eyes on me. Eyes on me.'

Kassia's back straightened. Her grip softened, just a little.

'I couldn't have done any of this without you,' Jed said at last.

'What? Ice skating?'

'No,' he said, their strides beginning to lengthen, their blades scoring a circle in the middle of the ice rink. 'Any of this.'

And as they retraced the beginning of their circle, her left foot slipped from under her and they fell spread-eagled on the rink, arms and legs a jumbled mess.

The air rushed out of Kassia's lungs and she swallowed deeply. 'Couldn't have done this without me, then?' she laughed.

Jed wasn't laughing. 'No,' he said.

They lay still for a moment, the heat of their bodies changing the top layer of ice below them into water that soaked into their clothes.

'Now we have this as well as Paris,' Jed said softly, turning eventually to help her up. 'Thank you.'

DAY 353
15th February

Dante had not been happy about Kassia and Jed's little adventure together. At least, Jed presumed he wasn't happy. Dante's signs had got larger and larger and faster and faster until eventually Jed couldn't bear to watch them, so he'd looked away. They had promised only to leave the boat again if they checked with Dante first and stuck to the schedule.

Jed didn't mind having to promise. But he didn't say sorry. And that night was the first time in months he'd slept soundly.

As he dressed the next morning, he rubbed his hand gingerly against his side. His ribs were a little sore from the tumble on the ice, but the discomfort made him smile.

Suddenly, Jed was aware of movement on the upper bunk.

'What the . . . ?' Charlie was sitting bolt upright, his hair a mess and his eyes wide.

Jed grabbed his T-shirt and wrestled into it quickly. He was annoyed with himself. He'd been so careful about hiding the scorch marks on his chest. 'Thought you'd left for work!' he snapped.

'Swapped to night shift,' Charlie mumbled, leaning over the edge of the bunk. 'Seriously, mate, what's the deal with those scars?'

Jed hesitated. He reluctantly lifted his T-shirt to expose his chest again.

'Whoah!' breathed Charlie. 'That's some serious scorching.'

Jed looked down at the raised burns. A dragon, in a circle. The ouroboros. But it wasn't finished. The mouth of the dragon reaching round for the tail, met only bare, unscarred skin.

'What's it mean?' Charlie stuttered awkwardly.

Jed let the edge of his T-shirt fall again. 'Eternal life,' he said quietly. 'Returning to the beginning.'

'And you've had that since . . . when?'

'Since Turkey,' said Jed. 'It came in sections. One part after each memory. But it's not finished.'

Charlie nodded thoughtfully. 'What if it *is* that simple?' he said.

Jed tucked his shirt into his jeans. 'Simple? None of

this is simple.'

'Just supposing, though,' Charlie said, launching himself from the upper bunk and standing so he was face-to-face with Jed, 'that the end of the journey is as simple as the beginning?'

Jed was more than a little unnerved by the intense way Charlie was staring at him.

'Supposing all that chasing around you did in Istanbul was part of the journey, not its ending?'

'I'm not following.'

'Supposing the race you're on ends where it started? Maybe that's how the dragon becomes complete. You go back to the beginning?'

'You get all that from some burn marks on my chest?'

'I'm a paramedic, mate. I specialise in reading signs on the body and making quick decisions!'

'If you're right about this,' said Jed, 'where does that take us?'

'Well, being a paramedic is all about precision,' Charlie added. 'No room for vagueness. You've been hunting all over London for clues. But maybe you've got to be more focused.'

Jed was still waiting for an answer that made sense.

'Where *exactly* did you start your journey?' asked Charlie.

'Beside the River Thames,' Jed said slowly. 'At St Paul's Cathedral.'

'OK,' said Charlie. 'Here we go.' He dropped on to the table every book he'd been able to find about St Paul's Cathedral in Church Street library. 'You can't just go bowling up to the place and expect to find the elixir, so you need to do some research.'

It was clear Dante agreed, but Jed could tell from his face that he was more than a little daunted by the mountain of books on the table.

'If the elixir is really at St Paul's, then we have to work out exactly where, so we can spend as little time out in public together as possible,' said Jed. He hoped his statement proved he'd learnt from Dante's lecture about being more careful, and that this would go down well. And Dante's face did seem to brighten as he reached for the top book on the pile.

'NOAH could be watching us,' added Kassia,

obviously keen to prove she'd learnt her lesson too. She reached for her own book. 'So time is important.'

'Actually,' said Jed, 'time is vital. I've been thinking about that.'

He could see his comment seemed a bit obvious to them. Everyone around the table knew they were chasing time. The fact that there were less than two weeks until the end of the year was something unspoken that stretched between them like a web. But he didn't mean it like that.

'There was a story, wasn't there? Back in Prague,' Jed went on. 'We thought everything we did in Prague was a waste of time, but now I don't think it was.' He hoped Kassia was remembering about how they'd had to literally use a mixture of blood, sweat and tears to get the final message in Turkey. 'I think everything Endel told us was actually a clue.'

'Endel?' asked Charlie.

'He's the old guy who knew loads about alchemy and sent us on this trail round Prague collecting signs. It didn't end well and we kind of thought that he was just messing with us. Delaying things until NOAH caught up.'

'He told NOAH where you were?'

Jed nodded awkwardly. 'He was working for them. The point is that what he asked us to do still gave us important information. About my memories and stuff like that.'

'So you trust this guy?' pressed Charlie.

'No!' snapped Jed. 'I think he was being manipulated by NOAH, but I also think there were things we found out in Prague we shouldn't ignore.'

'Like what?' urged Dante.

'Endel said alchemists used to keep their elixirs inside clocks,' Jed said. 'To make them stronger.'

Kassia put the book she'd been flicking through back on the table. 'What? I thought we worked out that the elixir might be at St Paul's.'

'We have,' said Jed. 'I'm just saying that what Endel said kind of confirms that.'

Now Charlie was looking thoroughly confused.

'St Paul's is sort of like a clock. It's a measure of time, anyway, as it was built to be three hundred and sixty-five feet tall to match the number of days in the year. So I'm just saying the architecture is important.'

Dante pulled a face and Jed wondered if it was because he'd spelt 'architecture' wrong as he'd finger spelled it in sign.

'The design of the building, I mean,' Jed signed more confidently. 'We thought we had to keep looking for symbols in London. And I think we're right. But, like you said about being a paramedic, it's all about precision now. Specific details, I mean.'

'OK,' said Charlie. 'I get you. Was there anything else you've been told along the way that might help too?'

'From Bergier, maybe?' cut in Kassia. 'If you think everything we've been told, as well as stuff we've seen, might actually be a clue.'

Jed remembered how in Paris they'd visited the old man who'd met Fulcanelli years before. What Bergier had said had taken them to Turkey, but maybe they'd missed things in what he'd told them too.

Kassia flicked through her notebook and found the statement from Bergier, which they'd written down months before. '*The phoenix man in the church resting on the edge of two worlds,*' she read aloud.

'So do we think there is a phoenix man in St Paul's?' signed Dante, before flicking through the pages of his book.

'Well, there was a Lazarus picture in Turkey,' said Kassia. 'The stories say he came back from the dead, which fits with the whole phoenix thing of coming back to life. So maybe there are pictures of Lazarus in St Paul's.'

'But doesn't phoenix mean coming back to life *after fire*?' said Charlie. 'I thought we were closing in on *specifics*?'

'Well, is there a fire connection with St Paul's?' asked Dante.

Jed scanned the index page of the book he'd taken and then flicked to a section near the beginning. 'It says here that the whole of St Paul's was burnt down in the Fire of London and had to be rebuilt. Reverend Cockren, that chaplain guy at St Paul's, told us that, didn't he?'

Kassia nodded. 'Yeah. I remember. Did anything survive the fire?' she said.

The four of them leafed through the pages of the books in front of them.

Finally, Dante thumped the table and pushed the book he'd been skimming towards them. He was gesturing to a particular picture. It was in black and white and showed a man with a pointy beard who was wearing a quilted ruff around his neck.

'Is that Shakespeare?' asked Charlie. 'Your famous writer dude?'

'No,' said Kassia, clearly trying not to react too defensively to the writer dude comment. 'It is a poet, though. He's called John Donne.' She looked at the text below the picture. 'He said some nice things like "no man is an island" and stuff like that.'

'Why d'you think Donne's important?' Jed asked.

'Says here,' signed Dante, 'that John Donne was the Dean of St Paul's before the fire.'

'And?'

'And he said something about phoenixes in this riddle, look.'

Jed read the text Dante was pointing to. He didn't really understand what it meant, but Dante was right. It did mention a phoenix.

> *'The phoenix riddle hath more wit*
> *By us; we too being one with it*
> *So to one neutral thing both sexes hit,*
> *We die and rise the same and prove mysterious*
> *by this love.'*

'I don't get the deeper level stuff,' signed Dante, 'but there's your phoenix.' He turned the book round so that he could see more clearly. 'And,' he added, 'it says that a statue of John Donne survived the Fire of London. Statues fit with your architecture thing. So I reckon, if we are looking for *specifics* now, he is totally our phoenix man.'

Kassia pulled the book round so she could see the section Dante had read from. 'You think that's it, then?' she asked.

Jed took a deep breath. 'I think it's piecing all the parts of the puzzle together. I think the elixir will be at the building that marks time, guarded by a phoenix man.'

'And that means what exactly?' pressed Charlie.

'I think the elixir will be at St Paul's Cathedral, hidden by a statue of John Donne,' said Jed.

It was evening. Victor looked across the desk at Reverend Cockren. The artificial light made long shadows on the walls of the chaplain's office, the light of the day long since faded. Victor took a mouthful of tea from the mug Reverend Cockren had just made him but he found it hard to swallow. Nerves tightened his throat.

The Reverend rocked a pen backwards and forwards on the top of the table. The noise of the metal against the wood made a sound like a clock ticking.

Victor put down the mug and reached for the bag that rested against the leg of his chair. He pulled out a small, flat rectangular package wrapped in brown paper.

Reverend Cockren nodded. It had been just over three weeks since he'd sent Victor the parcel in the hope of keeping the boy quiet for a while. Nearly a month since the frustration of their last visit when he'd tried to draw the boy's attention to the secret actually worth sharing. 'It is good you are a reader, Victor,' he said. 'It makes everything so much easier.'

Victor wondered if he really meant *everything*.

'Your father would have been very proud,' the Reverend said quietly.

Victor felt the muscles in his throat tighten even further. It felt impossible even to swallow air, let alone hot tea. 'I read it over and over again,' he said. 'But you might as well have it back. I didn't understand it.'

'Maybe not yet,' said Reverend Cockren. 'But thank you for the book's safe return.' He took the package and put it on his desk.

'You have done nothing except confuse me,' hissed Victor, wrestling inside himself. He wanted to shout. To beg again for clarity. He'd already done that, though. And all the old man had done was offered him a book of poetry.

'Perhaps that is true for the moment,' said Reverend Cockren. 'But everything will come down to choice, like most things in life do. It will be about which side we are on. About the roads we will travel.' He paused for a moment. 'Even if you don't understand yet, I think you see how complicated and important all this will be.'

An image of The Shard building flickered in Victor's mind. Tall and pointed and sharp, its tip like a blade.

Reverend Cockren smiled. He put his hand on the cover of the book. The pen stopped rocking and the room was silent.

Church Street Library

BOOKS, PROGRAMMES, CLASSES, & MORE
WWW.WESTMINSTER.GOV.UK/LIBRARY

RE

SOMERSET
HOUSE

SKATE AT S

ADMIT ONE

WWW.SOMERSETHOUSE.ORG.UK

WWW.SOMERSETHOUSE.ORG.UK

BUSES — London Buses

Route 6

38234   34234   23489

Fare: **Adult Single £1.5(**

Not Transferable
Valid From Stage: 2
Valid To Stage: 14
Orchardson Street, Little Venice
At: 08:50 On:

Route is Operate

Metroline

RETAIN TICKET
FOR INSPECTION

T PAUL'S
TH DRAL
400 YEARS AT THE
HEART OF LONDON

Ann Saunders

The Dream
BY JOHN DO
Dear love, for
ld I have
It wa
eason, n
fore tho
ream th
art so

As light
ine eyes
Yo
For thou
But when
And knew
When the
Excess
I must c
Profane

Comi
But ris

That l
'Tis m
If mi
Perch
Men
Thou
Will

ET HOUSE

00057

00058

絲綢路 Silk Road

There are times to stay put, and what
you want will come to you, and there are
times to go out into the world and find
such a thing for yourself.

ng for fa
ne wisely; yet
ot, but continued s
ughts of thee suffice
and fables histories;
thou thought'st it best,

noise w
hee
) an angel, at first sight;
sawest my heart,
ghts, beyond an angel's art,
hat I dreamt, when thou knew'st when
wake me, and cam'st then,
uld not choose but be
e any thing but thee.

ng show'd thee, thee,
ne doubt, that now
ot thou.
where fear's as strong as l
pure and brave,
r, shame, honour have;
hes, which must ready be,
t out, so thou deal'st with me;
ndle, goest to come; then I
hope again, but else would die.

DAY 355

17th February

Jed pulled the countdown chart from underneath his pillow. The paper was so thin now from refolding that it was almost transparent.

Eleven uncrossed days remained. Not months, not weeks, just days. Eleven of them. That was all.

Something weird happened to Jed's breathing.

He pushed the paper into his jeans pocket and joined the others out on the towpath. For the first time since arriving at *The Voyager*, they walked together.

It was morning. The sun had risen over the Thames, but its light was weak. Grey clouds skittered across the sky, some pierced by the top of the skyscrapers. The cloud was so thick it was impossible to see the tip of The Shard. The jagged points spiked blankets of grey and disappeared. The few people who were awake in the city did not look up. They lowered their heads and hurried onwards, looking down at the pavements, which shone with the traces of last night's rain.

Jed led the way.

He felt like he was about to walk across a tightrope and there was a very real chance that if he could make it to the other side, the answer he'd spent so long looking for would be waiting for him. But every step was a risk. The rope could snap. He could fall. And even if he completed the challenge, the answer could be missing.

'We just have to take it a step at a time,' Kassia whispered.

He wasn't sure he was brave enough.

Charlie walked with them as far as he could before he had to leave for the hospital. Kassia pressed a letter for her mum into his hand. Charlie had promised to hand it to Nat. Jed had insisted that she wrote it the night before. Kassia had argued. She had cried. When Kassia wasn't watching, Jed had cried too. But it was done now. An attempt at making sense of what made no sense at all.

The note explained that in less than a fortnight Kassia and Dante would be home. They did not know if Jed would be with them.

Charlie nodded as he left. 'Come back safe,' he said.

He hung back a moment, clearly wanting to say more but not sure exactly what. He stuffed the note for Anna in his pocket and pulled out the printed map of St Paul's he'd photocopied in Church Street library. Then he nodded again and left the three of them alone.

They walked for a while beside the Thames. Jed didn't look down at the water. Being so close to where he'd clambered free of the river nearly a year ago was terrifying. They'd come to St Paul's because they believed they might find the elixir where their adventure had begun. But maybe the beginning wasn't the cathedral, after all. Maybe it was the river?

Jed shook the thought from his mind. For the first time since leaving *The Voyager*, he looked up and held his gaze on the sky.

The dome of St Paul's looked back at him. A circular outline sweeping into the clouds. The top of the roof was hidden, like the tip of The Shard, its curve incomplete.

'Come on,' said Kassia, taking the map. 'Let's do this.'

The three of them walked up the path away from the river towards the cathedral.

Behind them, a street vendor was decanting flowers into buckets of water. In front, on the grass, was a circle of paving stones. And in the centre of the paving stones was a tall stone pillar with a bronze-coloured statue on top. A bust of a man with a pointy beard, looking away from the cathedral behind him, towards the Thames.

Kassia took Jed's hand and squeezed it.

'You OK, mate?' signed Dante.

Jed felt a constriction in his gut. 'I don't know,' he murmured. The constriction tightened, as if his insides were being squeezed in a juicer. 'I'm not sure. I don't think this is right. It doesn't feel right.' He was finding it hard to breathe. His eyes couldn't focus.

Kassia held on to his hand.

'It's a statue of a phoenix man,' signed Dante. 'Just like the books said. It's in the grounds of St Paul's. The elixir has to be here.'

Jed nodded, though he wasn't sure.

Kassia turned over the map. She'd scribbled notes from the books and she recited them aloud even though they'd read them a hundred times back in the narrowboat. 'The statue of John Donne was placed here in 2012,' she said slowly. 'Reverend Cockren was in the photo taken at the unveiling ceremony. This has to be the right place.'

They moved away from the flower seller and towards the statue. Underneath the figure, words had been carved. Kassia read them aloud too. '*Hence it is that I*

131

am carried towards the West; this day when my soul's form bends to the East.'

'What's all that about?' signed Dante.

Kassia clearly wasn't sure but she muttered something about how maybe John Donne had been confused and not sure which direction to look.

Jed put his free hand against the statue. The bronze was freezing against his palm. It made the cut in his life-line burn, the cold so bitter it produced heat. It didn't make sense. And he wasn't sure, now that he was here, that this made sense either. Could the answer really be this easy after all this time and all their searching? Months earlier, when they'd stood outside the Hagia Sophia talking about the poet Byron, Dante had insisted that poetry couldn't help them in their quest. The poetry book from Kassia's dad had surely just been a distraction too. But now Jed wasn't sure what to believe.

So much of what they hoped for now was resting on the poet, Donne.

'Well?' Dante signed. 'We need to do this quick while there's no one watching.'

Jed nodded. The three of them knelt by the plinth. They ran their hands along the base and across the paving stones that supported it. And then Jed's hand stopped moving.

One of the slabs was loose. The other stones butted together, carefully cut to complete the circle, but this one did not connect. The circle was unfinished.

Jed beckoned to the others. He eased his fingers under the lip of the stone, then lifted the edge as if the slab was a trapdoor. He raised it slowly, bracing his arm against the weight.

In the space below the stone there was a tiny hole.

Dante leant forward and took the weight of the stone, leaving Jed's hands free. Jed reached into the void.

His hands hit something solid.

A small bundle wrapped in oilskin.

There was no air in Jed's lungs. But in his hands there was a parcel, tiny and wrapped in cloth. It was much smaller than the package he'd found and then been driven to destroy at the top of Notre Dame. But somehow it felt just as heavy.

The sun glinted off the face of the statue and it cast light into Jed's hands. His fingers shook as he turned what he'd found over in his palm.

'Unwrap it,' urged Kassia, as Dante lowered the paving stone into position.

Jed unwound the cover, rolling and rolling the package in his palm until it was free of its protection. Jed dropped the oilskin and it fluttered to the ground, leaving what it had covered in the centre of his hand.

A tiny bottle, hardly bigger than the size of a man's thumb.

It looked so ordinary and so unimportant. The neck was chipped slightly, stoppered by a tiny cork that had been sealed into position with wax. The glass of the bottle was dull, thick and uneven in places, suggesting the bottle was very old. There was a roughness about the base. A tiny lip of glass protruded where the bottle had been snapped off a larger stem. This tiny edge of glass caught against the wound in Jed's life-line and new blood trickled across his hand and towards his wrist.

But Jed did not see the blood. He was focused on what was inside the bottle, moving as he tipped the precious container in his hand. This liquid was thick and pearly, and glinted gold in the tiny traces of light that still filtered through the clotting cloud. He'd seen liquid like this before. In his memory. A surge of recollections pummelled up from inside him. A huge black shadow grew and extended in front of his eyes. It darkened and thickened as it began to swirl, carving a circle in the air. The circle widened and expanded, growing a head and a tail and taking on the form of a dragon. The beast spiralled outwards, its head snapping and reaching for its tail making the dragon grow bigger and stronger so that it blotted out the sky and bored down on the centre of Jed's vision.

Suddenly, from the centre of the space created by the circling dragon, there was a surge of golden light like a fireball. It pulsed forward and engulfed Jed in its brightness and he shook, his fingers twitching protectively over the bottle in his hand. But that seemed only to drive the fireball inward. Energy surged along his arm and flooded his body, pushing out against his chest. His skin burnt. The scars on his chest tautened and puckered, forcing his body to crumple towards the ground.

Memories surged around him. *A darkened sky; a train careering from the tracks; bodies writhing in pain as poison choked their system; a throbbing wind that uprooted trees and finally a blazing heat that pressed down on him, making it nearly impossible to breathe.*

Thunder rumbled across the sky. This wasn't in memory. Neither was the fork of lightning which spiked to the ground, scorching a mark along the circle of paving stones where he knelt.

Jed closed his hand around the bottle of elixir. And then he closed his eyes.

Rain lashed from the sky, soaking Kassia's hair and her shoulders. She could feel Dante breathing heavily beside her. Jed was silent. He was totally still, his fingers tightly gripped around the bottle he'd unearthed.

There was no one else around. The few passers-by had hurried away to escape the rain, taking refuge in a doorway of the twenty-four hour café across the road. Only the flower seller remained, huddling under the canopy of his stall, speaking frantically into his phone.

'Take it, Jed,' Kassia wailed, the words stuttering in her throat. 'It's the last elixir! Take it now!' Her voice was frantic but Jed's eyes were still closed, his hand clasped so tightly round the bottle that the knuckles whitened in the rain.

'Jed, please! It's what we hunted for!' she pleaded urgently. 'Why are you waiting?'

Jed's eyes opened and the darkness from the gathering storm overwhelmed their colour, making them pools of inky black.

'Why are you waiting?' Kassia raged again.

If Jed took the elixir now, the hiding and the fear would be over. He would live for ever. The change he'd begun would be complete.

'Jed! Please!' She tugged his arm and he finally looked at her, his eyes the colour of midnight.

'I can't,' he said.

'Why?'

'It needs to be done right,' he said.

Dante was shaking his head in confusion.

'And I need to be sure.'

'Sure of what?' Dante shouted with his hands.

Jed's hand remained tight around the bottle, making his signing awkward and lopsided. 'On all the other elixir days, terrible, terrible things happened. Lives were lost. You know that!'

Kassia could tell he was looking far away and she guessed that the dragon bringing the memories had been circling in front of him, spinning and spinning as it had done in Turkey and in Paris when she'd seen what he saw and she'd felt what he remembered.

She did not see the memories now. Just Jed, his back braced against the beating rain.

'Supposing those lives lost were sacrifices?' mumbled Jed. 'Lives given up on the elixir days, so that I could go on living?'

'We've been through this,' insisted Kassia. 'The elixir and the deaths are not connected!'

'No man is an island!' Jed snapped back at her, quoting the poet whose statue gazed down on him. 'How can you be sure?'

'Jed, please!' Kassia could hear the flower seller. His voice was getting louder. 'Take the elixir!' she yelled, her own voice battling against the rain.

But Jed had no time to answer her.

Dante lurched forward on his knees and grabbed Jed's arm. He pointed behind him in the direction they had walked from the river. The flower seller had finished on the phone. But he had not stopped talking. He was no longer alone. Two men stood with him. A black boy with buzz cut hair. And a tall man with blond hair slicked tight around his head, the tails of his long, black coat flapping behind him like thick, leather wings.

This time there were no underground tunnels, no network of caverns and caves where they could hide, like there had been in Paris. They were out in the open and Cole Carter and Victor Sinclair had seen them.

'NOAH,' Kassia yelled.

The three men ran towards the cathedral, up the steps from the walkway and in the direction of the grass that skirted the statue.

'Come on!' yelled Kassia, grabbing for Jed's arm.

But he did not stand up. The rain lashed against his shoulders, his head still lowered, his hand gripped tight around the bottle of elixir.

'Jed!' Kassia's voice ripped from her throat. She pushed against the soaking grass and scrambled to stand. Jed turned, clutching at her arm now and keeping her still.

'Do you trust me?' he yelled.

'Jed! Please!'

The three men were getting closer. It would take them less than a minute to reach the statue.

'Jed! Please!'

'Do you trust me, Kass?' Jed yelled again, his voice fighting against the rain.

He'd asked her this before. In a time when she hadn't known about her father. When she hadn't known how Jed was involved.

'Kass! Do you trust me?'

The word clogged in Kassia's throat. But she knew she meant it, like she had done before. 'Always,' she said.

Jed released her arm and fumbled in his pocket. He took her father's watch and with his thumb he flicked its case open.

'The elixir is made strong because it's kept so close to the building that acts like a clock. It might weaken if we move it!' he said.

Dante grabbed for his arm but he pulled away. 'Jed! Please!'

'I'm sorry,' he said.

Jed swung the arm that held the watch behind

him, then crashed the watch face against the base of the statue.

Glass exploded from the casing. The face shuddered in the silver surround, before it fell on to the grass, cogs and wheels and workings from inside tumbling free.

Kassia's heart pounded against her ribs, like an animal trying to escape a cage. What was Jed doing? Why wouldn't he just leave? Why did he want to damage the watch?

Nothing she saw made sense.

Jed looked up at her and opened his other hand. Rain washed down on the tiny bottle, pressed tight inside his palm.

'Jed!' she yelled.

Jed was fumbling with the bottle. He was forcing it inside the protection of the watch casing.

He flicked the watch closed and the engraved swallow snapped back into position. The bottle of the last elixir was now hidden inside the pocket watch's silver casing.

Jed stuffed the watch into his pocket. He pulled himself up and grabbed Kassia's hand.

'Now we run,' he said.

The three of them charged away from the statue as the three men from NOAH raced behind.

Dante was leading. He glanced back, checking over his shoulder to see how close their followers were. But Kassia didn't want to see. She only wanted to run.

Jed gripped her hand so tightly she thought the bones would snap. Her feet thumped on the ground with every step.

They peeled round to the front of the cathedral, scrambling over the huge steps in an attempt to throw the men off. But Kassia didn't need to turn to know that they were still behind her.

There was a circular courtyard to the side of St Paul's. Pigeons pecked at the ground.

Dante led the charge through the middle of the flock and the birds lifted as if they'd heard gun shot, scattering as a thick, grey cloud. Rain splashed underfoot, driving in sideways, sharp and hard against her face.

A massive building to the right of the courtyard loomed over them. The London Stock Exchange. Two men in long black overcoats darted across their path towards the entrance, briefcases swinging from their hands.

Dante tried to avoid them but their heads were down, braced against the rain. And they were hurrying. Dante was so intent at looking over his shoulder, he didn't have time to change direction.

He ploughed into the first of the men as the second lunged to the side to avoid him. Dante's elbows drove into the man's stomach. The man doubled over, gasping for air, stumbling and faltering to keep his balance. He failed.

As he fell, the man tugged at Dante's side, trying to keep himself upright. It was too late, though, and they both hit the ground, rain splashing up from the puddles.

The briefcase burst open. Paper funnelled free, whipping upwards.

Dante scrambled to his feet. He waved his hands wildly in apology, but the man rolled on to his knees, he and his friend scrabbling desperately for the papers as they turned to pulp in the driving rain.

Dante's face was creased with concern. But they didn't have time to stop. Kassia could almost hear the beating tail of Carter's coat. The gap between them and their pursuers was getting smaller.

'I'm so sorry. So sorry,' Kassia yelled on her brother's behalf. The man did not hear her. His hands were clutching at the sodden pages, as pens from his briefcase rolled into the puddles.

Jed pulled her onwards and Dante hurried to join them. 'Left!' Kassia yelled. 'We need to take a left!'

They raced around the corner, charging in the

direction of the Old Bailey.

The High Court sat on the corner to the street they'd entered. A large white van was parked outside. The driver opened his door and walked quickly round to the back of the van, heaving the doors open wide. A policeman clambered out of the van. Another man was handcuffed to his arm and this man had a blanket over his head, covering his face. The prisoner walked unsteadily down the steps to the van as the policeman led him, a gaggle of reporters rushing forward from the shelter of the court's entrance, their cameras raised as they shouted, 'Did you do it? Did you work alone?'

The policeman and the van driver tried to force the reporters back as they herded towards the doors to the court. Flashbulbs fired. The rain flashed, illuminated by artificial lightning.

Jed stumbled around the back of the van, guiding Kassia out of the range of the reporters. He raised his other hand, shielding his face from the camera flashes. Kassia, too, lifted her arm and covered her face. The air tore open with bursts of light.

'Other side! Other side!' yelled Kassia, as she tugged Jed into the road and across on to the other pavement. There was no way they could risk being slowed by some over-keen reporter.

On the other side of the road, a lorry blocked the pavement.

A man and a woman were unloading enormous barrels from the back of the lorry and rolling them towards a trapdoor in the pavement. A worker from the Viaduct Tavern stood in the opening created by the trapdoor. He was taking the barrels as they dropped through the hatch and positioning them in the cellar.

More press had arrived to photograph the prisoner outside the court. A TV crew were unloading sound booms and a lighting rig from the back of a huge estate car.

The road was blocked. The pavement lined with barrels. And the men from NOAH were still following.

'Jump!' ordered Jed, charging towards the rolling barrel and letting go of Kassia's hand.

He cleared the barrel easily. Kassia too. But Dante's foot caught the outer rim, kicking the barrel sideways so it turned from its route towards the trapdoor's opening and careered instead into the wall of the Tavern.

The barrel shook. There was the sound of puncturing as a line of brick bit into the wooden strut work of the barrel.

Beer sprayed out of the hole, a plume of alcohol

gushing skywards.

The TV crew turned their cameras.

Behind them, Cole and Victor and the flower seller scrambled over the damaged barrel, beer mixing now with the rain that soaked them.

Kassia tried to remember the route back to Little Venice. Her head was thumping. She could hardly breathe.

'Straight on!' she signed, flinging her hand forward. It seemed the only option. The men chasing them had been delayed by the punctured barrel, but the gap was closing again.

'Go!' yelled Kassia, as the pedestrian traffic signal flashed green. 'Go now!'

They charged over the crossing and the signal changed to red behind them. Traffic streamed across the junction. Kassia could see Carter trying to dart between the traffic. A car blasted its horn. There was shouting. A thump of a hand against the bonnet of a car.

Maybe this was enough to stop them? But as Kassia glanced over her shoulder she could see the three men had cleared the crossing now and were still pursuing them.

Ahead, across the pavement like a gate, was an enormous wire shelving unit. It was taller than a man and as wide as a bus. And it was stacked with huge bags made of netting, which had been stuffed with footballs. A man stood at either end of the unit. Each was cursing the rain and trying to steer the contraption towards the delivery entrance to a sports shop. One of the wheels had caught in a pot hole. The unit was going nowhere.

Jed tried to dart around it, but the outer edge of the unit hung into the road. Traffic lined the gutter. There was no space to pass.

Jed looked frantically behind him. Back at the container that blocked his way.

Then he lowered his shoulders and charged forward.

Kassia tried to yell out but the rain was beating so hard against her face and her chest was so tight from the running that no words came.

Jed crashed into the bags that filled the unit. He tossed them forward and they tipped, bursting open and spewing footballs on to the pavement. Jed clambered through the gap created in the shelving and reached back his hand to steer Kassia and Dante through.

'Oi, son!' The older man at the end of the unit stumbled forward. 'What you playing at!'

Jed didn't answer.

The man stared through the gap in the shelves and

Kassia was sure he was going to climb through and follow them when Carter reached out and forced him to the side. Carter's face peered through the gap the fallen bags had created, and then followed after them.

Footballs rebounded across the pavement.

Kassia tried to avoid them but they rolled down the road like bowling balls in an alley. The balls overtook them as they ran, ricocheting off their ankles, thumping against them as if they were skittles at the end of the bowling lane.

Kassia kept her feet under her. She did not fall.

A road jutted out from the left. They crossed it quickly, racing forward.

'Is this the right way?' yelled Jed.

'I think so!' Kassia could hardly speak. 'University of Arts coming up on the left.' Her voice was rasping in her throat. 'But I can't keep going,' she pleaded. The blood was pulsing in her ears. Sweat itching on her forehead.

'You have to!' Jed yelled, grabbing for her hand.

A stitch was needling Kassia's side.

'I don't think I can.' She leant forward, pressing her hands against her ribs desperate to push the stitch away and drive more air down into her lungs.

Ahead, Dante floundered and then looked to his side. He pulled her towards the entrance to the university. The door opened. Dante tried to dart inside, but an officious-looking woman waved them back as two men stepped out of the doorway.

The men carried between them a huge canvas speckled with splashes of red and black. It had been covered in see-through plastic sheeting to protect the picture from the rain.

'Clear their path!' bellowed the officious-looking woman, slamming the door behind her.

Dante reached for the handle and tugged. The door was locked. They couldn't hide here. There was no way in.

The two men stepped down from the entrance. The picture blocked the road.

Dante, Kassia and Jed darted behind it. Maybe their pursuers wouldn't see them now. Maybe they would think they had gone inside the building.

There was shouting behind them. 'There! Still there!'

Kassia's feet thundered onwards. The men had not been fooled.

Suddenly, from behind them came a sound like an explosion.

Kassia looked back.

Carter had crashed his way through the painting. Wood frame and splintered canvas shrouded with ripped plastic was strewn across the road.

The woman was wailing. The two men shouting. But the men from NOAH were getting closer. The stitch in Kassia's side was growing sharper and more painful with every step.

'We have to keep moving,' Jed panted, although Kassia could tell that he was fighting for breath himself.

She howled and clutched her arm across her belly as they drove on towards Holborn tube station.

Suddenly, a swarm of people spilled up from the entrance to the station. The people were chanting and shouting and they carried placards sprawled with writing. Kassia didn't have time to read what the placards said. The crowd was clearly angry. They turned as one to the left, marching along High Holborn to where Kassia knew the road led into New Oxford Street.

'Merge!' yelled Jed, grabbing for a placard and weaving amongst the mob.

Kassia followed and wrestled her own placard from a middle-aged woman with dyed green hair tied up tightly in a bun. The woman smiled conspiratorially and launched lustily into the chorus of a protest song.

Dante joined the crowd in front of them, taking hold of the end of a banner that the protestors had strung from one side of the group to the other.

Kassia used her placard as a shield. It was difficult to see if the men were still behind them.

The protest song grew louder. A teenager at the front of the group shouted into a loudhailer and his voice crackled in the rain.

Kassia scanned the crowd, twisting and turning the placard as she marched. But if Carter and Victor and the flower seller were behind them she couldn't see them.

The throbbing in her ears lessened. The stitch in her side eased. She began to breathe more easily.

Until the road they marched along joined with another. And the group stopped marching.

'There!' yelled Jed, thrusting his placard back into the hand of the man beside him. Kassia knew the shout wasn't for the protestors. It was for her.

She dropped her placard and grabbed her brother's hand. The end of the banner fluttered free, dragging in a puddle. There was a roar of annoyance from the protestors. But there was no time to apologise. The men had found them.

Jed led the way, darting between the traffic when he could, now and then crossing on to the other side of the road. Kassia and Dante sprinted behind him.

The road widened. They had reached another junction. Kassia looked up and tried to get her bearings. They were outside the stage door of the Dominion Theatre.

The door swung open. A man dragging a clothes rail loaded down with costumes stepped on to the pavement.

Jed stumbled to a halt.

The flower seller was mere steps behind.

Jed grabbed the end of the clothes rail and tugged it from the stagehand. He spun the clothes rail round. The rail sliced the air like a scythe. Petticoats and crinolines flew off their hangers and fell like a blanket across the flower seller. He punched his hands to get free. Costumes wafted into the air, into the road and into puddles. The stagehand screamed, scrabbling to retrieve them, blocking the man as he tried to pass. 'Get out of my way!' the flower seller bellowed. The stagehand was having none of it. He grabbed the lapels of the flower seller and flung him hard against the wall. The man slumped over, sliding down the brickwork and landing in a crumpled heap on the soaking pavement. There was no way he would keep on following.

That left Carter and Victor. Two after three.

Kassia took over the lead. She could tell Jed was struggling. His face was red, his hair wet with rain and sweat.

'We can do this,' she roared. 'Come on!'

Their feet pounded the pavements, each of them urging on the others, as the gap between them and NOAH lessened.

When the traffic allowed it, they darted to the other side of the pavement, weaving down the street on one side and then the other until the road became Oxford Street.

'Inside a shop,' Dante waved frantically with his hands, hoping that they could get lost amongst the shoppers. But none of the big stores were open yet. It was too early.

Then Kassia saw a shopfront that seemed to be open. 'The Disney Store!' she yelled.

They darted once more between the traffic. Flags hung from the windows advertising a special promotion. But there was a security guard at the entrance. There was no way in. Suddenly, a balloon seller stepped out of the frontage. A cloud of Mickey Mouse balloons billowed after him.

It was too late for Kassia to change direction. The bunch of balloons was too huge to avoid. She ploughed into him, tangling herself in strings and helium Mickeys.

The security guard sprawled forward. Kassia wrestled to get free. Dante grabbed an escaped balloon and thrust it in the security guard's face. The man staggered, hands grappling to free himself from the string that had wrapped around him.

Kassia fought her way out of the balloons and grabbed for Dante's hand as he steered her onwards. Jed was just behind them. But so were Carter and Victor.

They raced past signs for Bond Street tube station. 'We need to head for Marble Arch!' Dante signed. 'Then turn right before you get to Bayswater Road!'

Kassia wasn't sure she would make it to Marble Arch! Her chest was burning. Air tore at her throat. She pummelled her arms, driving her feet down on the ground, rain splashing as she ran.

Eventually, Dante turned right on to Edgware Road. Surely there would be a large enough shop they could hide in now! But the road was lined with restaurants and few of them were open apart from a couple of small places serving breakfast. They couldn't hide in these. If they went inside they would be trapped! The only option was to keep on running.

Kassia saw a Waitrose store on her right. And it was open.

She waved across the road towards it. 'What d'you think?'

Jed looked uncertain. He was shaking, his arm

twitching, his face red-wine-coloured.

Kassia grabbed his arm and charged across the road. Dante followed.

Inside the supermarket, they were playing reedy music. An old lady was struggling to get a basket from the metal stand inside the door. Jed scrambled past her and grabbed a trolley. It was latched to the others and held fast.

'It needs a coin to release it,' gasped Kassia, fumbling in her pocket. 'But why do we—'

'Blend!' hissed Jed. 'We need to blend in.'

Kassia fumbled the pound coin she'd found and pressed it into the release part of the trolley handle. The trolley slid free. And they began to walk.

Kassia leant her weight against the handle as she struggled to breathe more slowly.

'Blend!' said Jed again, grabbing for a box of cereal and dropping it into the trolley.

They moved towards the back of the store, skirting along the end of each aisle, every now and then taking boxes and packages and adding them to the trolley. Jed gripped tightly. His hands still shook.

An announcement came over the tannoy. More assistants were needed at the checkout. The store was getting busier.

They moved slowly back along the end of the aisle.

'Have we lost them?' Kassia barely had the hope to whisper.

A mother was arguing with a small child about toothpaste flavours. An elderly man was handling each of the mangoes to check if they were ripe.

'I think so,' said Jed quietly.

And it seemed they had, until they entered the canned goods aisle.

Carter stood in front of them. His own trolley empty in front of him. Carter was obviously doing a less good job of blending in.

The aisle was empty except for them and him.

'Don't you think our little game is over?' Carter yelled, bracing himself against the handle of the trolley.

For Kassia, the game was far from done.

She yanked the trolley from Jed's hand and shoved it as hard as she could in Carter's direction. Shock registered on his face. In reaction, he pushed his own trolley forward. The two metal carts careered towards each other, their collision guaranteed.

Carter's trolley was empty. It had no weight to keep it stable. Kassia's trolley thumped against it, driving the end, turning it to the side and spinning the whole cart round so it was angled towards a towering can of baked beans. The trolley hit the base of the tower. The tower wobbled. The tins teetered. Carter launched himself forward to get out of the way.

But he was too late.

Cans crashed around him, cascading from the tower so that it slipped and fell entirely. A metal can struck him firmly on the head. He wobbled backwards, surprise still written in his eyes.

He collapsed against the tins of beans, slumping awkwardly on the floor.

An alarm sounded. The girl who had been arguing with her mother about the toothpaste began to cry. The old man in the fruit section dropped his latest mango to the floor.

Kassia, Dante and Jed raced towards the exit.

Carter was spread-eagled on the floor. The old lady was still struggling with her basket. But, turning the corner by the cleaning produce and charging out in the street behind them, uninjured and unstopped, was Victor.

'We have to outrun him!' yelled Jed.

'I'm trying! I'm trying!' cried Kassia. 'We need to turn left again!'

This road was wider. Traffic was heavier here. Dante was in the lead now, charging towards where the road dipped down and went under a flyover. Car horns blared. A taxi driver called abuse from the window. The rain thundered down. They did not stop running.

Victor did not stop chasing.

Finally, the road veered round again to the right. They were getting nearer to Little Venice. And Victor was still behind them. Kassia felt her muscles cramp. Her heart thundered in her chest. If Victor kept following, they would lead him straight to their place of safety.

As if thinking the same thing, Jed suddenly veered to the left again.

'We have to shake him off!' he yelled.

'But how?' cried Kassia.

Jed scanned back and forth and then steered them into a narrower street. 'There's no other way,' he said.

He turned his shoulder sideways and thumped hard against the garden gate of the house on the corner of the road. The gate swung open, cracking on its hinges.

'Jed! We can't!'

'We have to!' he yelled again.

Kassia turned. Victor was so close behind he could almost have touched them.

She followed Jed and Dante beyond the gate.

There was the sound of barking. A tiny terrier raced in circles as they ploughed their way through the garden. Jed bolted towards the back door of the house. He fumbled with the handle. There was no give. The door was locked.

Dante gestured at the garden wall.

'I can't!' wailed Kassia.

'You have to!' Dante signed.

He threw himself at the wall and swung his legs behind him, scrabbling to clear the top. Jed followed. Kassia reached up and tried to scramble over too. The terrier snapped at her ankles.

'Hurry!' Jed pulled her shoulders and dragged her up.

She was balanced on the top of the wall when they heard Victor throw himself against it. He was fast. Quicker than them. He was snatching at the pocket of Kassia's coat.

She kicked out.

Victor yelled. He staggered backwards. His sleeve caught on the thorns of a bush and he tugged his arms free, discarding his jacket so it hung there like a flag.

Kassia crashed over the wall to the other side.

'Come on,' yelled Jed, grabbing for her hand.

There was no sign of Victor. The kick must have winded and disorientated him. And it had won them time.

They scrambled through the flower garden and vaulted over the next wall, with Dante following. This wall was easier for Kassia. She was getting the knack.

As Dante cleared the barrier, Kassia heard Victor's

breathing once more. He was gaining ground again.

In the next garden there was a line of washing, hanging dripping in the rain. Jed and Dante tugged down handfuls and lobbed them behind them in an attempt to slow Victor. But he knocked them from the sky, undeterred.

Kassia could see over the next wall. There was one garden beyond it. And this one edged the canal.

There was no way out. Water one side. Victor the other. He had hunted them down and he had caught them.

They cleared the final wall.

And Victor faced them.

Then Kassia saw it. A plank resting on the top of the nearest canal boat. It acted like a gangway from the garden to the boat.

'You have to stop your running, Fulcanelli!' Victor bellowed, his arms spread wide in victory.

But Kassia had no intention of letting Victor catch them.

She grabbed hold of the end of the plank and tugged it free from the top of the narrowboat. It took all her strength to keep her steady.

Victor wasn't looking at her. He was looking at Jed.

And so he had no time to steady or prepare himself as Kassia swung the end of the plank towards him.

It hit him in the stomach with a sickening thud. She saw the breath rush out of his lungs as he gulped for air.

It was only then that he turned to look at her, and she did not understand the look he gave her.

It was almost as if he was surrendering. Allowing the momentum of the plank to move him without resisting.

Soundlessly, he reeled back from the garden, his arms open wide, the tattoo of a unicorn in chains rippling like water on his skin. He wavered for just a second, his eyes locked on Kassia's.

And then he fell, crashing like a stone into the canal.

'What? Stop looking at me like that!' Kassia's voice bounced in rhythm with her running.

'Like what?' Jed asked, striding to keep up with her.

'That!' she said, frowning.

'I can't help it. You were pretty impressive back there.'

Kassia shrugged and floundered a little. 'I didn't want him to catch us.'

'Obviously!' laughed Jed. 'There was no arguing with you and your plank!'

Kassia frowned again and Jed could see that she was

blushing. 'Yeah, well, I saw the opportunity to slow Victor down. So I did.'

'Kind of odd, though, don't you think?' Jed said, glancing over his shoulder to check they really weren't being followed. 'That he didn't jump out and keep chasing us? As if he'd kind of done what he needed to.'

'Yeah,' said Kassia. 'You don't think . . .'

'You didn't kill him, Kass. He made it to the side of the canal. He just, I don't know. Maybe he knew he was beaten.'

'Well, he deserves everything he gets after what he's put us through in the past.'

Jed nodded. 'You stopped me dealing with him in Prague,' he pointed out.

'That was different! You looked like you wanted to kill him then. I just helped him into the river.'

Jed nodded again. The thought of what could have happened to Victor in Prague if Kassia hadn't stopped it still troubled him. Jed had been so close to the edge of something really dark and Kassia had pulled him back. And now she'd saved him yet again.

'Thank you,' he said, trying to increase his pace to close the gap between them.

'Any time,' she said. She looked away, clearly regretting the mention of time. The word felt somehow forbidden between them. They ran on without talking after that, trying hard to keep up with Dante, who was by now some way ahead.

As they rounded the turn in the path, Jed was sure that he'd never been so glad to see a narrowboat.

Dante was already on the deck of *The Voyager*, unzipping the screening. He turned to help Kassia up, then grabbed Jed's hand. The three of them tumbled inside.

'I don't know about you,' said Jed, making straight for the fridge, 'but I could do with—'

'Jed!' Kassia's voice was sharp.

'Something to eat and—' He grabbed a bowl of cold rice and a plate of spring rolls.

'Jed!'

He blew out a breath. OK she'd saved him and dumped Victor in the river, but surely Kassia could just let him know what she wanted to eat. He leant his weight on the fridge door and stood up properly. And then the rice and rolls clattered to the floor.

'Giseppi? How? What? Why?' The questions tumbled over themselves.

The Frenchman sitting at the table smiled. He gestured to his companion, Amelie, who was at that moment tangled in an elaborate hug with Dante. 'I have the thinking,' said Giseppi jokily, 'that some of you are very pleased to have the seeing of us.'

Jed strode across the room and clamped Giseppi in his own hug. Kassia followed his lead and, after a while, Amelie finally released Dante so that they could hug her too.

'How? Why? I don't understand,' Jed repeated.

Giseppi raised his hand, batting away the words. 'Let's have some of your British tea,' he said, 'and I can do the answering of your questions.' He leant forward and added more seriously, 'And perhaps you will do the answering of some of mine.'

Jed made drinks while Dante and Kassia took seats round the table. There was plenty of room for him when she'd finished, as Amelie and Dante were taking up barely more than the space of one person on the bench.

'How did you get away from the authorities in Paris?' Jed asked.

Giseppi sighed. 'There was only so long they could do the keeping of us just because we'd been in the catacombs.' He looked across at Amelie. 'It wasn't too bad in custody. But they have done the clearing of the Court of Miracles which is not good.'

Jed ran his thumb awkwardly along the top of his coffee mug. The steam scalded his skin. 'I'm sorry. I never meant to bring you all this trouble.'

'I know,' said Giseppi matter-of-factly.

'How did you find us?' signed Dante, as Kassia translated, although Amelie made it clear from the way that she watched Dante's hands, that she at least needed no help with reading his words. It struck Jed how unobservant he'd been not to notice the way Amelie and Dante felt about each other in Paris. But then the time in the catacombs had been painful. There had been a lot he'd missed.

'The Brothers of Heliopolis,' said Giseppi. 'That is how.'

Jed knew that Giseppi was a descendant of one of the original Brothers of Heliopolis who had worked with Fulcanelli to make the elixir. And he knew that Giseppi was himself a modern day Brother. But that didn't explain how Giseppi and Amelie had made it to London, and to Little Venice, and to the exact narrowboat where the three of them were hiding.

Reading Jed's questions from his expression, Giseppi took a mouthful of tea, then put down his mug and began to explain. 'The Brothers of Heliopolis are connected through time and across the world. Our job has always been to track you down, Fulcanelli. And to protect you so you can do the completing of your quest.'

Jed pushed his hand into his pocket and gripped tightly to the silver watch, resting now within the folds of the countdown chart. 'How did you know where we were?'

'The network of Brothers does the stretching like a golden chain,' Giseppi went on. 'Between Paris and Prague, and Istanbul and London. Surely you have seen that?'

Jed *had* seen that. But the point of his question was how had Giseppi known to come here? To *The Voyager*?

'The Brotherhood did the alerting of us to your return to London,' Giseppi went on. 'And, after quite a lot of the persuasion, your uncle and someone called Charlie at the hospital sent us here.'

'You didn't hurt them?' demanded Kassia.

Giseppi looked confused. 'There was no hurting. Just explaining. And some showing of some loyalties.' Giseppi rolled up his sleeve and patted the tattoo mark of the Brothers of Heliopolis on his arm. Jed thought of the mark of NOAH on Victor's arm as he'd flailed into the water.

'So the Brotherhood let other Brothers know what's going on?' pressed Jed.

'Of course. You think it was a coincidence that I found you for the first of the times on the Phoenix train?' laughed Giseppi.

'Phoenix,' whispered Jed.

'Excuse me?'

'Phoenix,' Jed said again, a little more loudly. He remembered the name of the train that had carried them from Prague to Paris, on the same day that Giseppi just so happened to be travelling with Amelie to the Festival of Fools at Notre Dame. 'I get it now. Wow, it's all connected. I didn't realise.'

'You have something to tell us about the phoenix?' said Amelie, speaking for the first time and moving her hands almost fluently in sign.

Jed nodded.

He took the watch out of his pocket and opened the casing. The golden liquid glinted inside the ancient bottle that rested in the lid. 'The phoenix led us to the sixth elixir,' he said.

Giseppi splashed his tea on the table in surprise. 'You've found the last elixir. And you haven't done the taking of it yet?'

Jed closed his hand back over the watch and snapped the casing shut. 'NOAH were after us. We managed to lose them. Throw them off our trail for the time being.'

'So take it now!' urged Kassia.

'I – I can't rush this,' Jed stuttered.

'Rush?' Giseppi's face was creased in confusion. 'Haven't you been doing the hunting of this for nearly a year? And time before that, even? Since you took the fifth elixir?'

Jed knew this was true. Knew it should have been so easy just to drink the final dose. But it wasn't. Something was stopping him. 'I need to be sure,' he said. Even to his own ears that answer sounded stupid. The way those seated round the table looked at him made it clear none of them understood his reasoning either. He grappled around for another argument. Something he could say that would help them understand.

'I'm not sure how it will work,' Jed mumbled. This was true. Maybe the final elixir would work differently from the others he'd taken. Maybe, after all this time, it wouldn't be effective. Or maybe it would hurt. It wasn't his pain he was scared of, though. 'I don't know what will happen,' he said. Somehow the hope and promise that everything would be OK had seemed stronger than the reality of taking the elixir now and finding out.

Everyone around the table stared at him.

'There are only eleven days left!' Kassia's words forced their way through her teeth. 'Why are you waiting?'

'This isn't just about me!' Jed said, staggering away from the table. He tried and failed to channel some of the energy that surged inside him into pacing. The walls of the narrowboat pressed in. The ceiling felt too low, as if a great weight was being forced upon him. There wasn't enough air. 'On the days when I took the elixir before, bad things happened. Very bad things. And how many people are there in London?' He spun round to face them. 'Eight million? Ten million? And you expect me to do something that I know could hurt people.' He thumped his hand on the table and the mugs jolted. 'I need to be somewhere far away. Somewhere the risk is smaller.'

'We can do that.' Giseppi stood up from the table. 'Get you somewhere quiet. Away from NOAH. I have the answer to both problems.'

'Really?' said Kassia hopefully. 'You're going to take us to another underground world?'

Giseppi clapped his hands. 'Eat something. Get some sleep. Then do the packing of some clothes,' he said. 'We leave London late tomorrow afternoon.'

'Where are we going?' pleaded Kassia.

'To a bigger world of water. I think you will be the safer there.'

DAY 356

18th February

'He's taking us "off-grid",' said Kassia, following Jed up the tube escalator and whispering to him as they climbed. 'What does that mean?'

Jed took a deep breath. 'Well, out of London for a starter. Though when I asked him if he meant out of the country, I didn't understand his answer.'

'And that "world of water" stuff?' pressed Kassia, beeping her card on the gate machine and following the signs that led to the main part of St Pancras station. 'What do you think about that?'

'Not a clue,' said Jed.

Kassia stuffed the ticket back in her pocket and hoisted her bag on to her shoulder. She couldn't force down the feelings of nerves that bubbled inside. She was trying really hard not to get cross. Trying not to completely lose it. Her palms were red where she'd gripped her hands into fists so tightly. She didn't understand what was happening.

There were ten days left.

Ten days until the elixir stopped working. Ten days before Jed would die. Why didn't he just open the bottle and drink it?

What was there to think about? Everything they'd done over the last few months; everything they'd given up and risked, was about finding the elixir and now he had the very thing that had driven them onwards and he just wouldn't get on and take it! None of this made sense. There was no proof the elixir and disasters were connected. No proof there was a link between the elixir and people getting hurt. And what about *her* pain? What about the fact that something clawed at her insides every time she looked at Jed and imagined him not being there?

'Are you sure we don't need passports?' Dante signed beside her, jostling forward as they queued for train tickets.

Kassia hurt too much to translate and so Amelie did it instead.

The necklace of shark teeth round Giseppi's neck rippled as he turned to face them. 'No passports needed.'

'But you're taking us out of the country?'

Amelie translated again.

'That I am,' said Giseppi.

Kassia folded her arms. Why did everything have to be so complicated? She was seriously in danger of exploding with frustration.

Suddenly, she was aware of a hand against hers. Dante smiled at her, and carefully he spelt out single letters on to her palm. 'T-r-u-s-t t-h-e-m.' The final shape of the letter M needed his fingers to lock around her hand. She bit her lip and let him hold on longer than was necessary for the spelling of the word.

Once the tickets were bought, Giseppi led the way across the concourse. The display at the end of the platform said the final destination of their train was Broadstairs. This seemed a pretty random destination, and, as far as Kassia knew, it was still in England.

'Seriously?' said Jed, as Giseppi opened the door to a carriage near the end of the train that looked fairly quiet.

'We get off halfway,' said Giseppi. 'I suggest you get some rest. You do the lookings of being very tired.'

Kassia almost laughed. She hadn't slept a wink last night. Tired did not come close to how she felt. And once she'd sat down and the train started moving, she felt her eyelids drooping.

POEMS

JOHN DONNE

PETALS FOR

FLOWERS FOR
ALL OCCASIONS
2 Goldhawk Road

FORMERLY
ELI WHITTLES

SEND FLOWERS
ANYWHERE

No. 2014

SEND TO Mrs Michael Brown

ADDRESS 11 Bernard Roads U642

NAME

DESCRIPTION

Hand Bouquet

35

CHARGE TO Mr B.K. Parutti

MESSAGE You are a unicorn

5 00

£35.00

NOAH

WE DELIVER 24/7

D. @ S P's

But she wanted answers. She wanted action. She wanted . . .

Dante put his hand on her knee. 'Trust them,' he signed again into her open palm.

And so Kassia closed her eyes and surrendered to the rhythm of the train.

About an hour passed before Kassia was aware of Jed rocking her gently awake. She sat up, aware she'd let her head rest on his shoulder as she'd slept, and painfully aware too, that she had drooled. She wiped her face with the back of her hand. 'Have you taken the—'

Jed grabbed her hand. 'Shhh. Not here.' She looked up and saw that the carriage was more crowded than when they'd pulled out of St Pancras. 'This is our stop,' he said, helping her to her feet.

She shook herself, though it was only when they'd stepped off the train and on to the platform and she'd been blasted with the cold February air that she felt fully awake.

'This is it?' she said, looking up and down the tiny platform. It certainly wasn't London any more.

'It's on the way,' said Giseppi, winking and leading them through the rather smelly underpass and on to the station forecourt. 'Try and do the keepings up,' he added. 'We want to catch the tide.'

Kassia shivered. She liked this idea less and less. But if Jed was sure he needed to be somewhere with fewer people in order to take the elixir safely, then they were on target.

They hurried along Pier Avenue and then down on to Central Parade. A pier jutted out in front of them, but Giseppi turned and led them past a large public garden in the direction of a clock tower. Kassia didn't look up at it. The thought of clocks made her hurt again.

There was a line of coloured beach huts edging the shingle and Kassia thought for one minute that perhaps Giseppi had one of these in mind for their next hiding place. But he strode past these in the direction of the harbour wall which curved round in the direction of the pier.

Suddenly, he stopped. 'OK,' he said brightly. 'Time for the explainings.'

He pointed to a small boat moored beside the harbour wall that was set apart from a range of other boats. All of these looked more substantial than the battered thing Giseppi was gesturing towards.

'You want us to hide out on that?' said Kassia, regretting at once the fact she'd taken her brother's advice about trust and given up the warmth and safety of *The Voyager* for another boat which didn't even have a roof, let alone any beds to sleep in. 'You have got to be kidding me!'

'No,' said Giseppi. 'I am not doing the kiddings. And you are not doing the stayings on this boat. It is just a way of making our trip to safety.'

Kassia looked across the choppy grey water. 'France?' she yelped. 'You want us to sail across to France on that thing in the middle of February? How will that be safer than London? Are you out of your mind?'

'No,' said Giseppi, in a way that made it clear that he was rather enjoying Kassia's frustration.

'You said you were taking us somewhere out of the country and you bring us to the sea and point to a boat. So where else can you be taking us?'

Now Giseppi laughed openly. 'I am taking you to Shivering Sands,' he said.

'And where on earth is Shivering Sands?' Kassia blurted.

'It's in Sea Land.'

Kassia wrapped her arms around herself and looked up at Jed. 'He's joking, right? He has to be making this stuff up?'

Jed laughed too, though his laughter sounded all wrong and was tinged with sadness. 'No,' he said quietly. 'None of this is made up, Kass. This whole thing is actually happening.'

She looked out to the sea and tried to stop herself shaking from the cold.

'Come on, then,' called Giseppi, as he clambered down the shingle and towards the sandy stretch where the boat was moored. Amelie and Dante hurried behind him, hand in hand. Kassia glanced at Jed. She wondered for a moment if he was going to take her arm, but he pushed his hands into his pockets instead and walked down the beach. She followed, her own hands balled into fists.

Once at the boat, it was necessary to move it along the sand, as the edge of the sea was a few metres away. The five of them formed a semi-circle round the stern and pushed hard. There was quite a lot of resistance. The waterlogged beach sucked at their feet, trying to drag them downwards. Eventually, the boat hit the water and began to float.

Giseppi loosened the mooring rope and jumped aboard. He held out his arm and helped each of them clamber in. By the time it was Kassia's turn she had to wade almost waist deep in the sea. The cold bit at her legs. Her shoulder wrenched in its socket as Dante and Giseppi heaved her aboard.

Kassia flopped on to the bench next to Jed, but she

didn't look up at him. She watched Giseppi as he grabbed the tiller and took a long cord connected to the outboard motor and wrapped it round his wrist. 'What's that?' she blurted.

'How you say?' mumbled Giseppi, searching for the right word. 'The kill switch. If we go too fast or do the hitting of a problem, this will stop us.' He nodded reassuringly, then fiddled with the motor, pulling another long cord from the centre so that the engine thrummed into life.

'Ready?' Jed said. She could feel him bracing himself on the seat beside her.

The question sounded ridiculous. She was ready. But why wasn't he? Was he being honest with her?

For a moment the boat just bobbed up and down on the water as white horses charged towards it and broke on the prow, drowning out the chug of the engine.

'He knows what he's doing,' Amelie said gently.

Kassia wondered if she was talking about Giseppi or Jed.

The boat nosed forward, topped the wave and angled out from the harbour. The sky was growing darker. And the sea churned black below them.

They followed the line of the pier out from the shore and beyond the finish of the harbour wall. The helter-skelter on the end of the pier was silhouetted with lights that flickered in the splash of the waves. Kassia gripped tightly to the edge of the boat.

As the helter-skelter passed behind them, Kassia could just make out a strange platform sticking out of the sea, on the horizon. A curved boarded walkway swept like a semi-circle around it.

'What's that?' called Kassia, raising her voice so she could shout into the spray.

'The landing stage,' said Giseppi. 'I have the thinking it was separated from the rest of the pier by a storm.'

Kassia did not want to think about any storms. 'Is that where we're aiming for?' she yelled.

Giseppi waved his hands. 'No. No. That is not the Shivering Sands.'

'So where are we going?' Kassia asked for what seemed like the hundredth time.

'Our destination,' said Giseppi, 'is nine miles out in the ocean.'

DAY 357

19th February

It was dark. Kassia held the lamp Giseppi had given her to try and illuminate the water, but the waves were so large that they threw the boat around, making it difficult to keep the light steady.

Jed's eyes stung with spray from the sea. His shoulders and chest felt tight as he battled his own cramped muscles as well as the ocean. He had believed that Giseppi knew what he was doing, but now that the boat was being tossed so violently about in the water Jed's faith in his friend's plan was ebbing away.

Amelie called out behind him. 'There. Can you see now? To the left.'

Kassia twisted where she sat. She held the lamp higher, its beam bending against the water.

Jed had expected to see a shoreline. A beach; some houses, perhaps; or maybe a harbour. There was nothing like that.

Instead he saw huge, rusty iron girders rising out of the sea like giant pillars.

'Onwards,' called Giseppi, a note of relief mixed with his command. 'Doing the landing may be difficult.'

Landing where exactly? thought Jed.

And yet, as the boat edged closer and the light settled, the structures became easier to see. The pillars were, in fact, humongous legs. There were lots of them, arranged in groups of four. Each set was topped with an enormous, rusty, cube-shaped building, and there were windows in each building, although these were tiny. In places, a cable had been strung across the water from one building to another. Ladders led up from the water level between the legs of each building to a trapdoor, which obviously allowed access.

'Is this some sort of prison system?' called Kassia, swinging the lamp so that each metal wall was picked out with light.

'They are sea forts,' said Giseppi.

'Who do they belong to?'

'Oh, they were owned by your government in the war,' Giseppi said. 'But as they are in the international waters they are not really part of your land.' He pointed to the cabling running from one to another. 'These forts have been used in the past by the – what you say – pirate radios.'

'Pirates?' gulped Kassia.

'I have the meanings that the radio stations were not official.'

'These places are used by radio stations now?' said Kassia.

'Oh, no. These forts are long empty. And so, like the Court of Miracles in Paris, they are a place of safety for those who are in the need of hiding.'

'Do you know every secret hiding place there is for people in trouble?' asked Jed.

'I know many worldwide,' Giseppi laughed. 'But this one will do us for now.'

He gave directions to guide the boat between the legs of the nearest fort, stopped the engine, and then took the mooring rope and attached it to a rusty hook on the huge metal pillar.

'Now we have done well to not take a swim in the ocean,' he said. 'So I am thinking you all need to do the being careful as you climb.'

Jed was totally sure he would be careful, though he wasn't sure his arms would have the strength to pull him up the ladder. But the thought of sitting a moment longer in the freezing boat drove him onwards. He checked he had the watch safely in his pocket, hoisted his bag on to his shoulder, then stepped on to the ladder.

Kassia was already in front of him. She looked behind her only once, checking she was being followed, and he tried to smile, but his face was so cold that it was difficult to move his mouth properly and he thought it probably looked more like he was grimacing. Kassia seemed to speed up her climb and so before Jed knew it they had reached the hatchway that led into the fort.

Beyond the ladder was an open-slatted staircase. The light from Kassia's lamp just about illuminated the sea between the gaps in the steps but, at least unlike the ladder, these stairs had proper handrails. Jed took a moment to catch his breath. But Kassia was moving forward with the light and so he had to plough on to keep up with her.

Once at the top of the stairs it was easy to see that the inside of the fort was vast. Rooms led from one into the other, each of them packed with various pieces of damaged furniture. There were beds in some rooms, tables and chairs in others, and in one, some type of ancient radio system and a pile of vinyl records.

Giseppi took the lamp from Kassia and led to the corner of the room where there was a fridge-like contraption, which Jed guessed was an electricity generator. He flicked some switches, fiddled with a few dials and then, when nothing much happened, he gave the thing an almighty kick. There was a whirring noise, several loud thumps and a high-pitched whine. Then a gentle chugging, and the fort was filled with light.

'Better,' grinned Giseppi. 'Things always are when you get rid of the dark.' He took a deep breath. 'You did the wanting of somewhere quiet, Fulcanelli. Somewhere the risk of hurting people was lower. I think you will agree I did the findings.'

Dante was over by the window gazing out towards the sea. 'How long can we stay here?' he signed.

'As long as we have the need,' said Giseppi.

The answer was almost funny. How could any reply not make reference to the days that remained? Nine of them. They'd sailed nine miles into the ocean. They had nine days left before the year was up. No one said the number aloud again or in sign, because it stretched between them, not like a web any more, but like wire. Barbed wire.

'There is plenty of space here,' said Giseppi. 'The fort was used by one hundred and twenty men at a time. We can have a room each,' he said brightly. 'Although, just like in the Court of Miracles, it might do us better to stick together and do the staying in one room.'

'Food? And drink?' signed Dante.

'If my sources are right, there will be the canned goods and bottled water,' said Giseppi. He looked around hopefully at a large cupboard balanced precariously against the wall, strode towards it and yanked the door handle. The hinge was rusty and it took several tugs to get the door open, but just as Giseppi had predicted, there were rows of cans and bottles stored inside. None of it looked particularly appetising and Giseppi clearly sensed that no one was that thrilled by what they saw.

'It is not the fault of me if you have grown used to take-away Chinese food,' he said, trying to make a joke.

Jed remembered the fallen rice and spring rolls and his stomach grumbled.

'In a few days I will sail back to Herne Bay to get us the more supplies,' Giseppi added. 'We have enough for now.'

'Great,' said Jed, aware as he spoke that his voice sounded a little too loud. 'This is great. We'll be safe here. While we make decisions.'

It suddenly felt as cold as it had done on the boat, and Jed looked at the ground. Until *he'd* made a decision was what he really meant. Panic tumbled inside him like a boat tossed about in a storm.

When he looked up, Kassia was staring at him. He noticed that her hands were still clenched into fists.

oyster®

18+

Discount expiry date

Alexandra Piros

Issued subject to conditions - see over

'I just don't understand.'

The tiny bottle of golden elixir sat on the table between them. Jed was sitting and Kassia was standing. This allowed her to pace and she was doing a lot of it, backwards and forwards between the table and grimy windows that looked out to sea.

Dante, Giseppi and Amelie were somewhere out there on the ocean, having taken advantage of a calmer day to sail back to Herne Bay and get more supplies. It was far from calm where Jed and Kassia were. The air was icy and it felt like a storm was roiling.

They'd skirted round the issue of the elixir for three days. But there had been no proper discussion. Now, in the middle of nowhere, the two of them alone, Kassia had made it clear she wanted to talk about it. And it was equally clear to Jed that there was absolutely nowhere he could hide.

'There's under a week left, Jed,' she spluttered. 'That's six days. Less than a hundred and fifty hours. Do you *get* that? Do you understand?'

He flinched from her words and watched the golden liquid swirl inside the bottle, lifting and stretching, always on the move, changing as he watched.

'Just tell me why you haven't taken it?' she pleaded.

Jed looked at the bottle. To Kassia's credit, she wasn't reminding him of how they'd given up so much to get to this point; that they'd fallen from hot air balloons; splashed through sewers; been plunged into rivers; and even been tested with poison. She didn't mention any of this. She just asked why.

His mouth couldn't form the words he needed, though, because his brain wasn't clear about which ones he should use.

'Please!' she urged. 'I just don't understand.' She stopped her pacing and stood in front of him. She pressed her hands down on to the table and her eyes locked on his.

'Because I'm scared,' he said at last.

She pulled back, as if this of all the answers he could have given wasn't the one she had expected. Something in her face softened.

'Of what?' she asked quietly, pulling out the chair

from behind the table and sitting down.

He fumbled again for words that would make sense to her. But most of all to him. 'I've told you,' he whispered. 'It's why we're here, miles away from anybody! How do we know about the cost to other people if I take it? The disasters from before? What if they happen again? What if they happen to *you*?'

She reached across the table, her hands close to his but not touching. 'I don't think it's connected,' she said. 'We've been through that.'

'But nothing about any of this has been coincidental, has it? Giseppi and the Phoenix train; the phoenix man; the cathedrals. There's a golden chain that links everything, and what if the final link makes more terrible things happen? What if more lives are lost because it's the last dose? Many more lives than before? And even if we're here, as far away from crowds as we can be, supposing . . .'

'I don't think there's a connection,' Kassia interrupted.

'Because you don't want there to be!' he blurted. 'Like you didn't want to see the truth inside my memories.'

His words stung her. 'But we've done what you wanted!' she said. 'How could you drinking that hurt anyone on land?' She gestured wildly at the bottle.

'We can't be sure.'

Kassia bit her lip and confusion turned itself into something stronger, bubbling up behind her eyes.

Suddenly something snapped inside him. '*You* take it then!'

Kassia's face reddened in shock.

'You take it,' he said, pushing the bottle across the table so that it was close enough for her to touch.

'Don't be crazy!' she fumed. 'I haven't taken the other doses!'

'Maybe this one is so strong on its own that it will work for you,' he said, pushing the bottle even further forward.

'You're being ridiculous,' she said, getting up from the table. 'And you're not being truthful with me. You go on about the truth, and me not seeing what really happened in the memories. But I'm not the one who's lying. You are! Tell me the real reason you won't take it! What are you really scared of?'

Jed pressed his hands to his eyes, as if maybe shutting Kassia out meant he wouldn't have to face what she was asking.

She leant forward and grabbed his hands, forcing him to look at her. 'Tell me!' she cried.

And so he said it. The truth that had churned and twisted inside him since the statue at St Paul's, possibly even before. 'Maybe living for ever isn't such a good idea.'

Kassia let go of his hands. She folded her own arms across her chest. And then she nodded.

Jed wanted to make her understand what he was saying. This wasn't just about him. This was about her too. But her face told him that having begged for answers, she wasn't ready to hear more.

'Maybe it will only work on the final day of the year,' he offered desperately. 'Maybe I have to wait. Maybe it's set up like that.'

'Maybe,' she said quietly.

'Kassia, please.'

'It's OK, Jed. I understand now.'

He lurched up from the table, the elixir in his hand. 'No, you don't. I—'

She turned her back on him and walked towards the window. 'There are a lot of maybes,' she said. 'So you're right to wait.'

'Kassia, please. It's not what you think.'

'How do you know what I think?' she said so softly that he could barely hear.

'That I'm waiting because I don't want to be with you?'

'*Is* that why?'

'No! Please. You have to—'

'I don't have to do anything, Jed. I've done everything to help you because I *wanted* to. Not because I *had* to.'

Jed couldn't look at her. He scrabbled with the casing of the pocket watch and slipped the tiny bottle inside its place of protection. Then he pushed the watch back inside his pocket.

'You have the answers, Jed. Not me,' Kassia said.

'I don't have answers, Kass. Just questions,' he said. 'All I want is to do the right thing.'

She stepped slowly towards him. Her eyes focused directly on his and she did not look away. When she spoke her words were slow and deliberate. 'I'm so angry.'

Then she turned and walked out of the room and closed the door.

Jed stumbled towards the wall to stop himself from falling. He wrapped his arms around himself and the pressure made the scars across his chest burn. He leant his back against the wall and slid downwards until he was sitting, hunched over on the floor. He held his head in his hands and listened to the sea throwing waves back and forth against the base of the fort.

Carter increased the zoom option on the laptop screen. The red dot blinked on and off, pulsing like a heartbeat.

Montgomery leant in to get a better view. 'Clever,' he said. 'Very clever. But – ' and he laughed as he finished his sentence – 'not clever enough this time.'

'We're totally sure?' said Carter, snapping the laptop closed.

'We will make sure,' said Montgomery, twisting the end of his walking cane round and round in his hands as if he was tightening a screw. 'One hundred per cent certain.'

Hours passed. Jed was unsure how many.

He'd given up trying to think. His mind had lost all hold on the thoughts that buffeted around inside his head like the pounding waves outside.

There was a clicking sound. The door swung open. Kassia stood in an arc of artificial light.

Jed stumbled to his feet and pulled himself up to standing. She walked towards him. Then she reached up and kissed him on the cheek.

Jed closed his eyes. As she pulled away again she whispered three words. 'I'm sorry, Jed.'

The room was silent.

And that meant they heard the noise of a boat docking underneath them and footsteps on the stairs.

The door reopened. Giseppi, Dante and Amelie stepped inside.

But they were not alone.

Victor and Carter were standing either side of Giseppi. More men stood behind on the stairs. They were completely outnumbered.

Instinctively, Jed pulled Kassia towards him, standing in front, making himself a barricade between her and NOAH. Even in that moment of panic, when he saw that three men guarded the door, he knew two things clearly. He had to keep Kassia safe. And he had to protect the elixir.

He dug his hand into his pocket, drew out his watch and fumbled it into the pocket of Kassia's coat.

'I couldn't stop them,' pleaded Giseppi.

Anger raced through Jed's veins. Had Giseppi led NOAH here? Had he betrayed them like Endel and Jacob?

'Oh, now don't you go getting angry with your friends from the sewers,' Carter said, the edge of his leather coat flapping behind him. 'I know it's easy to think that perhaps he is the one who sold you out. But you'll find it was someone much closer to your circle who brought us here.'

Jed looked across at Dante but his arms were open wide and he was shaking his head.

Carter laughed. 'Even closer,' he sneered.

Jed felt all the air rush out of his lungs and he was

sure he would throw up. 'Kassia?'

'No!' she yelled. 'Jed, I would never—'

Of course she would never betray him. How could he believe a single word NOAH said? Then Jed replayed the words Kassia had whispered just seconds before. 'I'm sorry.' For what? For this? For leading NOAH to him?

Carter was moving forward, his arms even wider, the tail of his long black coat skimming the floor, lifting clouds of dust in its wake. 'Oh, I know you want to trust her, Fulcanelli.'

Jed's mind was in free-fall. Had Kassia betrayed him with a kiss?

'But ask yourself this,' Carter ploughed on. 'Do you think she can really forgive you after what you did? After what happened to her father? Do you think anger like hers can ever truly be forgotten?'

Anger? The word bounced inside his mind. She'd said she was angry. Dante had said she was trying to hide it. But she'd told him, only hours before, that she was. The words rang again in his ears. Was she angry enough to betray him? Angry enough to abandon him to NOAH?

'Ask yourself this, Fulcanelli. Has she ever left you? Has she ever looked at you in disgust and walked away? In London? In Paris? In Turkey? Has she ever given up on you before?'

The answer to Carter's question was that she had. Three times.

Memories crashed together in his brain. The flat on fire in Fleet Street. Jacob's fall from Notre Dame. The Dark Church in Turkey. Three times he had let her down and three she had given up on him. He had been so sure she had forgiven him. Was that because it was what he wanted to see? Had all this been a trick? A way of getting her revenge?

'Jed, please. I'm telling the truth!'

So this was about honesty, then. But hadn't everything about the last few days proved that honesty was complicated? Had he been honest with her?

He spun round to face her.

'Jed, please.'

Carter was enjoying this. He stared at Jed, relishing his discomfort. Jed could hardly breathe.

'How many times have you let her down, Fulcanelli?' Carter snarled. 'Didn't you think there would be a chance that eventually she would let you down too?'

Kassia stumbled forward. 'Jed. I'm not perfect but—'

Jed didn't hear the rest of what she said. Fear and confusion surged inside his mind, like a wave that lifted him and flung him against the shore, grinding his face into the shingle on the beach. He saw nothing clearly, heard only the roar of his blood inside his ears.

When he turned at last to look at her, Kassia lowered her eyes and looked away. Was that guilt? Relief they'd tracked him down? She hung on to Jed's arm. Somehow everything hurt too much to push her from him.

Carter was laughing. 'Touching, isn't it?' he said, looking back at those who stood behind him, as if he was at a party and wanted other people to join him on the dance floor. 'How the prey doesn't recognise the trap we set for him.'

Bile surged in Jed's stomach. His vision flickered so all he could see was out of focus. But there was no black dragon swirling and circling in front of him. Only Kassia, her face creased in confusion, or maybe satisfaction. He had no idea what the truth was of what he saw.

Jed pulled away from Kassia's side. And then he ran.

He ploughed straight for the three men at the doorway. They recoiled in shock, snatching to grab him. Jed had no fear now. And nothing to lose. He launched himself against them and they reeled like bowling pins so that he burst through them and out the other side.

The rooms in the fort were interconnected, leading one from another. And three days of exploring gave Jed the advantage over those who followed. He careered from room to room, slamming doors behind him, driven by the need to get away. By more than that, even. A rage that swelled through every fibre of his being.

Doors slammed behind him, torn open again by those who followed. Jed picked up an empty packing case and hurled it hard across the room behind him. It hit the first chaser in the upper body and the wood exploded into splinters. The man cried out with pain.

But there were still two men chasing Jed.

Jed ripped the next door open. The room that had been used as a radio station. He yanked the soundboard from the wall and flung it behind him, wires waving like the tentacles of a demented jellyfish. The second chaser jumped over the debris, charging forward. Jed grabbed for a stack of vinyl records from the floor and hurled them behind him like weaponised frisbees. One hit the man squarely on the forehead and his legs buckled under him, sending him crashing into the wall.

Two chasers neutralised. There was only one left now, but he was gaining ground.

Jed charged into the connecting room. There was

no furniture or clutter here apart from a desk and an office chair on wheels. He ducked behind the door and tried to quieten his breathing.

The man crashed into the room, skidding to a halt, scanning left and right in confusion. Jed reared forward, taking the office chair and shoving it as hard as he could towards the chaser. His legs buckled too and the ground slid from under him.

This man was stronger than the other two. He would not be so easily thwarted. He scrambled up, and loomed above Jed, his face wet with sweat, his shoulders braced.

There was just the desk between them.

Jed lowered his head and stampeded forward. With all the strength and anger that he had, he rammed the desk against the chaser's stomach. The man staggered. He flung his arms back against the window behind him, extending them like he was pinned to a cross.

The window, which had been weakened by the salt from the sea, shattered. The chaser's torso broke through and hung out over the ocean.

Jed could hear shouting in the rooms behind him. If the others had tried to hold Victor and Carter back, then they had failed.

Beyond the doors were the stairs.

Below the stairs was escape.

A voice called out from the window. The chaser, half-in, half-out of the buckled opening, about to topple into the sea.

A man about to fall. Like Jacob from Notre Dame.

Jed looked again towards the stairs.

He heard the swish of Carter's coat behind him.

The man yelled out again.

Jed rushed to the window and pulled him back inside the room, allowing his body to crumple to the floor.

In that moment, he felt a blinding pain in the back of his head.

And everything went dark.

AM 54 60 70 80 100 120 160 KC
FM 88 90 93 97 102 108 MC

FM

FM AM

GOLDEN SHIELD

DESICCANT

...is a
small jellyfish
found in the
Mediterranean Sea and in the
waters of Japan. It is unique
in that it exhibits a certain
form of "immortality": it is
the only known case of an
animal capable of reverting
completely to a sexually
immature, colonial stage after
having reached sexual matur...
as a solitary stage.

DAY 361
23rd February

Jed felt water splashing on to his face. The cold took his breath away and he reared up, blinking his eyes against the light. There was a sharp pain through both his wrists and he fell back again.

He tried to pull himself up once more. But the same pain at his wrists forced him down.

He screwed up his eyes and the face peering at him swam into focus. Montgomery.

'Hello, Fulcanelli. It's been a while.'

This was true. Though it felt like only yesterday that the head of Department Nine at NOAH had claimed to be a friend, and then thrown Jed into a cage.

He wasn't in a cage this time, but on a boat. Perhaps the same one that they had used days ago to get to the fort. The boat was rising and falling in the waves, and as Jed looked around he could see that the fort was slipping away from them on the early morning horizon.

He fought to sit up. Pain in his wrists drove him back again. And in his confusion he saw that his arms had been chained.

'Let me go!' he yelled.

Montgomery laughed. He leant forward, bringing his face even closer to Jed's, and he laughed, his eyes flashing. Then he sat back in his chair and tapped the walking cane he held against his knees. 'That would be a no,' he sneered.

Jed made a growling noise that burst from somewhere deep inside himself.

'You think we would take risks this time?' said Montgomery. 'You really think that after all this time and all this energy, we'd risk you getting away. Again.'

Jed bit his lip.

'Oh, you have led us a merry dance, Fulcanelli! I have to applaud your determination.' Montgomery rested the walking cane on his knees and began to clap slowly. 'All that stuff in Paris! The chaos you left behind in Turkey. And then your oh-so-clever hiding in London. I have to admit that you have tested us to the limit! Some would even say you have made us look a little foolish,' he snapped. 'So the answer is a definite and unequivocal "no" to your request. We have no intention of letting you go this time.'

Jed turned his head. Water on the bottom of the boat slopped against his cheek.

Montgomery reached forward and pulled Jed's face around. His eyes locked on his. 'None of that matters now,' he said, the tips of his fingers hard against Jed's skin. 'We have caught the man who will live for ever and there is no chance that we are going to let you escape.'

Unable to pull away, Jed closed his eyes.

'Look at me!' yelled Montgomery, his fingers pressing harder. 'You will look at me when I am talking to you!'

Jed's eyes flickered open.

'That's better. It is, after all, only polite.'

Jed bit his lip again.

Montgomery nodded, took a breath and then withdrew his hand, drumming his fingers along the walking cane with a speed that matched the rhythm of Jed's heart.

'There is one thing you can help us with,' Montgomery said slyly.

There was no way that Jed was going to answer him and Montgomery knew this so he went on with his request.

'I need to be sure.' He took the cane in his left hand

and drove it down sharply on to the bottom of the boat. 'You see, Fulcanelli, it was always, always about surviving the Flood, wasn't it?'

Jed's head began to spin. He tried not to think about his sister and the flood that claimed her life. But the image of the rising waters and then her grave rose up from the darkest corners of his mind and he felt an anger he hadn't felt before surging inside him. He hoisted himself up and he didn't care that pain tore through his muscles. 'Let me go!' he yelled.

Montgomery took another breath. His voice was clipped and precise. 'Oh, I'm sorry. Have I reminded you about Zoe? That's awkward.'

'Let me go!' Jed yelled again.

'You think when I talk about the flood that I mean Paris, don't you? Oh, Fulcanelli, when will you learn that I am concerned with a much bigger picture than that?'

Jed fell back to the bottom of the boat. Water splashed around him.

'I mean *the* Flood,' Montgomery said. 'Because this story – ' he checked himself – '*your story* has always been about the unicorn escaping as the waters rose. But, you see, you have confused us with your exploits and we need to be totally sure that what we have captured in you is the unicorn we've hunted. You understand our problem, don't you?'

'You're mad?' Jed snarled.

'No, no,' said Montgomery. 'Not mad. Just keen to be sure.' He leant forward. 'Time was never on our side before. Heidelberg and the poison; the explosion in Turkey. There's a chance, you see, and, granted, it's a tiny chance, that you escaped death each of those times, through luck or accident. Your friends, after all, survived a tumble from a hot air balloon. So you can't blame us for wanting to be convinced.'

'Let me go,' Jed said again.

'We will,' said Montgomery, 'if you are not the unicorn.' He laughed. 'So let's get the flood to show us once and for all if you are, shall we?'

Jed felt the boat jolting. It had hit against something and people behind him were hurrying to keep it steady, mooring it, probably. Jed wrestled to turn so that he could see. Hands pushed him down.

Other hands tampered with the cuffs attached to the chains that held him. But they were not disconnecting the chains from him, only from the side of the boat.

Suddenly, someone hauled him upwards, forcing him to stand. He was face-to-face with Carter. Neither of them looked away.

Carter held on to the chains and he dragged Jed

to the prow of the boat.

It quickly became obvious that the boat wasn't at shore, as Jed had hoped. Instead, it had been moored to a huge wooden pillar which plunged down into the sea.

Jed recognised the place from their journey to the sea fort. It was the landing stage that had been separated from Herne Bay pier.

Above him, a swooping, dilapidated wooden platform curled round in a semi-circle. Beside the mooring posts, other wooden pillars pushed down to the seabed, keeping the landing stage afloat.

'What are you doing?' Jed mumbled, as Carter dragged him by the chains, out of the boat and along the tiny wooden walkway that looked as if it must be used by fishermen when setting off from the landing stage.

'Your final test,' laughed Carter.

They had reached another wooden pillar and Carter tugged the chains so that Jed was forced to his knees. He looped one end of the chain and locked it together, anchoring Jed to the post.

'Get in the water,' said Carter.

'Don't be crazy!' Jed shouted. 'I'll drown.'

Carter laughed again, and then he looked across to where the boat they'd clambered from bobbed on the water. Montgomery stood, watching them, leaning on his stick. And he was laughing too.

'You don't have to play this game with us, Fulcanelli,' Carter said. 'Now I'm asking you nicely, get into the water.'

Jed tugged against the chain. 'You're mad!' he yelled.

'Maybe,' said Carter. 'But you're the unicorn. And we're going to prove it so there can be no debate. Now, if you won't get in of your own accord, then maybe I should help you.'

'Please don't do this,' Jed begged.

Carter was growing impatient. He shoved Jed hard in the shoulders. Jed plunged from the edge of walkway into the water.

The cold took his breath away. His lungs squeezed, fighting for air.

Pain seared through his arms and his shoulders.

The chain kept Jed's arms above him. The only way to keep his head above water was to kick wildly with his legs. 'Let me go,' he spluttered, gasping and turning as waves licked at his chin and he strained his head upwards.

He couldn't hear the answer from the landing stage, nor the answer from the boat. Water splashed in his ears.

He drove his feet downwards, kicking and scrabbling, trying desperately to find some support on the landing stage that he could rest his weight on. But there were no ledges below the water. The post just drove downwards to the bottom of the sea.

Gulls circled above, screeching and calling.

The muscles burnt in his shoulders. The cuffs dug into his wrists.

He fought with all the strength he had.

But the tide was turning. The sea level rising. Water splashed into his mouth, salt stinging the back of his throat.

If he could just rest a moment. If he could just take in more air.

Suddenly, a wave crashed over him and he sank below the surface.

Blackness closed in.

He plunged his feet down, his back grazing the pillar.

And he heaved himself upwards, gulping in air that tore at his lungs.

The waves were relentless. They dragged him under again. Pressure crushed in his chest. His eyes flickered and blinked against the dark.

Once more he pushed himself up. A flicker of light. A flash of sun against the waves.

And then he fell, down and down into the water. The muscles in his arms screamed against their restraints, but the chains held fast. And the weight of the sea pulled him down.

His feet stopped moving. His back slid against the post. The light of the sun slipped away. Until all was dark again. And all was still.

Finally, the water billowed above him. He no longer fought against it.

Carter hauled Jed from beneath the waves. He laid him on the walkway and tugged the chains around his wrists until he was standing.

Jed spat salt water from his mouth. Carter didn't even flinch.

'Amazing,' Carter said quietly. From the boat beside them, Jed heard the sound of clapping.

Jed turned. Montgomery was standing in the boat. His face was beaming. 'Absolutely incredible,' Montgomery said.

Jed shook his head and water ran from his hair and pooled at his feet, staining the wood of the walkway dark like it had been drenched with blood.

'We hoped with everything we had that it was so,' Montgomery went on. 'Now, *finally*, we can be certain.'

Jed stared at the floor.

'You were underwater for over thirty minutes,' Montgomery shouted. 'And so there can be no doubt at all. No room for disbelief.' He drove his stick against the bottom of the boat and it sounded to Jed like a judge banging his gavel in court just before he declared his verdict. 'You are the unicorn, Fulcanelli. We have hunted you throughout the years. And now – ' Montgomery took another breath – 'our hunt is over.'

"SCANDINAVIAN SE

G. N. STEARNS
New York Agents, HUBBARD

87
86
84 83
82 81
80 79
78 77
76 75
74

NOAH

Spire
Levels 75-87

The View from The
Levels 68-72

idences

DAY 365

27th February

The next days blurred into a muddled mess. After the boat came a car journey. Then nights, maybe two or three, Jed couldn't tell, spent inside The Shard. They used the cage again, though this time Victor did not arrive to let Jed free.

Unlike the last time he'd been captured, they asked no questions.

There was a rota to ensure someone was always watching him. Carter paced the room as Jed sat slumped against the bars of the cage. Montgomery sat on a stool, tapping the end of his walking cane against the floor. The woman, who Jed remembered was called Martha Quinn, stood with her back against the door frame. She did not take her eyes off him.

When the frustration flooded up inside him like the waves that had overwhelmed him, Jed charged at the bars. 'What do you want with me?' he bellowed.

They told him nothing.

'All in good time,' said Montgomery. 'There are things to set up.'

If Jed's calculations were correct, there was no time. No months. No weeks. Only days . . . Before the chance to take the elixir was over.

Finally, they unlocked the cage.

A guard fastened Jed's wrists together with metal cuffs. He was taken to a small room where he was fed, and they allowed him to wash. His clothes had been laid out for him. On top of the trousers, taken from the pocket, was a small folded piece of paper. It had been bleached by the sea, the writing faded, but the marks still visible.

'What is that?' asked the guard. 'Some sort of diary?'

Jed shook his head. They still didn't know, then, about the need for the sixth elixir. As far as they were concerned, Jed was immortal, his eternal life guaranteed.

The guard threw Jed a pen. 'You're behind,' he said, gesturing to the countdown chart. 'It's February the twenty-seventh.'

Jed stared at him.

'Well, go on, then,' the guard sneered. 'That game is obviously important to you.'

Jed took the pen and, with shaking fingers, he made new crosses on the page.

That was it, then.

Not months. Not weeks. Not days. Hours. Less than twenty-four of them.

Between life and death.

Jed screwed the paper into a ball and dropped it. As the sun rose over the city, he and the guard rode the lift in silence to the ground floor.

There was a car waiting. Jed was bundled into the back. It wasn't the same car that had taken him from Kassia's home months before. Then, he had believed these people had claimed him because they wanted to look after him. Now he knew better. Now the windows of the car were blackened and it was impossible to see the view.

Eventually, the car stopped.

Montgomery twisted round from the passenger seat. 'Don't make a scene,' he said quietly. 'It's not in your interest.'

Jed looked away. The car door opened and the cold February air hit him in the face.

Looking up, Jed could see that they were outside the Houses of Parliament. 'Why here?' he said.

Montgomery stepped out on to the pavement, leaving room for the two minders who stood one either side of Jed, their shoulders pressed against his as a reminder about the need to obey.

'The Palace of Westminster is appropriate for our needs now,' said Montgomery. He leant forward, his weight on his cane. 'You're the unicorn, Fulcanelli. This isn't just about science any more. NOAH has never acted alone. You don't think those who run the country have ever been far away from our quest for truth, do you? How do you think all the tracking was possible? The passport checks? The international links?' He laughed, mocking Jed's naivety. 'The knowledge you will give us requires legislating. We need to govern your grasp on eternal life. We have to put laws in place to ensure that the secret you give us is managed and controlled. You didn't think, did you, that we would let your story reach the ear of the masses? What you tell us will give us power. We need power to control that.'

He led the way towards the parliament building and Jed and his minders followed.

There was a network of corridors, stairs and passageways. It was clear to Jed that they were somewhere in the basement, below the line of the River Thames which he knew was beside the building, making its way towards the sea.

Finally, Montgomery stopped. In front of him was

a set of enormous double doors, which reached from floor to ceiling.

Montgomery lifted the handle and pushed the doors open. They led into a huge room that was nearly empty of furniture except for some benches, a table and seats at one end and a line of chairs at the other. There were no windows, the only light came from a massive chandelier that hung from a mottled blue ceiling decorated with painted stars.

'What is this place?' Jed asked.

Montgomery spun round, his arms open wide, cutting his cane through the air. 'They call it the Star Chamber. Rules and decisions are made here about complex and difficult matters. And I think, Fulcanelli, you would agree that you are a somewhat difficult matter.'

The minders led Jed towards the back of the room. There was a single chair separate from the others, in front of a desk covered with wires and hardware. Victor and Carter stood behind the chair.

Carter turned Jed round and unfastened one cuff from around his wrist. He used a small metal key to disconnect the chain that kept the cuffs together. He passed the loosened metal cuff to Victor, pushed Jed round and into the chair, then linked the chain around the arm of the chair and used the key to fasten it back tight to the single cuff.

It was only as Carter moved away that Jed realised other people were entering the room. A long line of men and women dressed smartly to attend a very important board meeting. And in the middle of the group was Kassia.

Jed's stomach flipped over. Why was she here? Was her betrayal so complete that she was working with NOAH now? Had everything she'd done and said since he'd returned to London to find her been a lie? And before that? Had everything they'd been through been about this moment? He couldn't look at her.

Kassia was struggling between the men who walked either side of her. 'Jed!' she cried. 'I didn't lead them to you.'

That had to be a lie. How else had they found them? They'd been off-grid. Giseppi had made sure of that. There were no cameras in the middle of the ocean. No chance for face recognition or tip-offs, however involved the government was. NOAH had to have been led to the sea fort. There was no other answer that made sense.

'Jed, please. You have to believe me!'

He remembered what she'd said days earlier. He didn't *have* to. But every part of his being *wanted* to.

Montgomery laughed. He stepped into the middle

of the room as those from NOAH took their seats along the back. 'Wouldn't it be wonderful if you knew the truth about that?' he said, flailing his stick through the air again. 'Because, after all, it is the truth we all seek now.'

'Jed!'

Jed looked away.

On the wall he saw a clock. It was eight a.m. There were sixteen hours left until the year since he'd clambered from the river was over. Sixteen hours. That was all.

Carter put down the key to the cuffs and fiddled with the cables sprawled across the table. He took two thick wires and linked them round Jed's chest. Then he took a tubular plastic sleeve and strapped it over Jed's arm, which was chained to the chair. He lifted Jed's unchained arm and made Jed put it on the table, attaching thick velcroed bands around Jed's first and third fingers. Wires ran from the bands to a small black box attached to a laptop computer.

'What is all this?' Jed asked.

'A way of ensuring honesty,' said Carter, blowing a bubble with his chewing gum and letting it pop against his lips. 'We used the submersion technique to establish the ultimate truth. Now we are concerned with details. We had the sneakiest suspicion that there was a chance you might not work with us as we wanted. So drastic times, lead to drastic measures.' He fiddled with the end of the wires and then took a seat behind the laptop so he could see the screen. 'We're all set,' he said to Montgomery. 'Whenever you're ready.'

'Oh, I've been ready for years!' smirked Montgomery.

'Wait!' said Jed, scanning the line of people at the back of the room, his eyes darting quickly from Kassia's and along the row of suited spectators. 'Dante, Giseppi, Amelie? What have you done to them?'

'Don't get yourself upset,' said Carter, looking up from the screen. 'Your friends are safe. We left them in Herne Bay so they are extending their little holiday.' He made a snorting noise. 'We made sure they had no money and no way of getting back to us. But their goodbyes to the one who betrayed you were most touching, weren't they, Viccy boy?'

Victor didn't answer.

'I didn't betray you, Jed!' Kassia yelled from the back.

Montgomery's face wrinkled in annoyance. 'You will refrain from shouting out, Miss Devaux!' he snapped. 'Your rejection of the truth is useless and you will be ejected from the chamber if you cannot be quiet!' Then his face brightened a little. 'Now, let's get down to business, shall we?'

The laptop Jed was attached to made a buzzing noise.

'This is a lie detector,' Montgomery went on. 'And so we want to add one truth to another.'

He took a deep breath and rapped the end of his cane, hard, against the floor. Jed flinched as the sound echoed round the chamber.

'We know you are going to live for ever,' Montgomery confirmed. 'And now, Fulcanelli, you are going to tell us how.'

Jed's hand twitched on the table. He felt the plastic sleeve tighten on his arm, sensing that the thing had been inflated with air. The laptop obviously had some way of measuring his blood pressure. And whatever was connected to his fingers and across his chest was being used by the computer to measure other reactions. He tried to slow his breathing. But his heart was hammering, the wires pressing against the unfinished dragon made of scars.

'So, first question, Fulcanelli,' said Montgomery, striding across the space in the middle of the room. 'How did you make the elixir?'

'I don't know,' Jed mumbled, the inflated sleeve pressing taut around his arm.

There was a clicking noise from the computer.

Carter studied the screen as lines of black ran horizontally across it. 'He's telling the truth,' Carter said.

Montgomery balked. It was obviously not the answer he had hoped for. But neither was it the only question NOAH wanted answered. 'Where is the recipe?' Montgomery said.

The sleeve tightened again on Jed's arm. His fingers twitched. 'Destroyed,' he said. 'It was in Paris but I burnt it.'

Another clicking noise from the computer. Horizontal lines streamed across the screen.

'The truth,' said Carter.

Montgomery sneered. But he did not stop his pacing. 'Simple yes or no answers, Fulcanelli.' He looked along the line of those watching and, encouraged by their silence, he asked another question. 'Is there more elixir?' he said.

Jed's breath fluttered in his throat. What could he say? How could he tell them? After Jacob? After he'd seen what wanting the elixir could lead to? 'No,' he mumbled.

The computer clicked. Lines spiked vertically across the screen. 'He lies,' said Carter joyfully.

There was excited muttering amongst the spectators. Jed tried to flex his hand, but the connections on his fingers kept his palm flat against the desk.

'Is there more elixir in London?' pressed Montgomery.

Jed looked across at Kassia. Her eyes were wide. Did she have it? Was it still hidden in her coat?

'No,' Jed mumbled.

A clicking. Vertical lines spiked across the screen.

Muttering from the crowd. Montgomery stood still. His eyes were narrowed, as if he was running through the story of the boy from the river and honing in on his target.

'We know you made a visit to the cathedral,' he said carefully. 'Is St Paul's connected to the elixir?'

Jed tried to breathe. The elixir was no longer there. Surely this reply was safer. But his head was thumping. He was so confused. 'No,' he said.

Clicks on the computer. A wave of lines across the screen, stretching across as well as up and down.

'He lies again,' said Carter, staring hard at the screen.

Montgomery nodded. 'Yes or no answer, Fulcanelli. 'Did those who made the elixir for eternal life hide it at St Paul's?'

Jed felt his stomach fall inside him. Sweat beaded on his forehead. For some reason he did not understand, he knew he had to protect the cathedral.

'No,' he said. His voice was weak but the spike of the lines scoring up the screen was strong and indisputable.

Carter smirked. 'The elixir is at St Paul's,' he said.

Montgomery's face broke into an enormous grin. 'This is better than we hoped,' he said. 'You can lead us to the elixir and we can replicate the recipe and make as much as we need.' The crowd behind him murmured in agreement.

Jed's heart was straining against his ribcage. The scars pulled so tight he was sure they would tear. The elixir wasn't at the cathedral. Kassia had it. And he'd got just fifteen hours now to get it back and take it. He yanked his arm against the restraint.

Montgomery drove his cane down on the ground. The noise echoed and the crowd hushed to silence. 'You will lead us to the elixir, Fulcanelli. We will be reasonable with you. We have all the time in the world, so you will have the time you need to search.'

The lie of this statement burnt in Jed's ears.

Montgomery twisted the top of the cane. 'You will find it, wherever it is hidden in that building. And you will bring it to us. Then we will share the secret of eternal life with exactly those we choose.'

There was clapping from the people seated at the back. Carter switched off the laptop and disconnected the leads from Jed's fingers. Jed felt the air seep out of the plastic sleeve around his arm, mimicking the escape of air that seeped now out of his lungs. What would he do? He hadn't got time to go to St Paul's. And what would happen when NOAH realised the elixir wasn't there?

If Kassia had the elixir and she'd betrayed him, why hadn't she just handed it over to them? NOAH hadn't got the elixir from Kassia. So surely that meant she was telling the truth. But if that was the case, how did NOAH find them in the middle of the ocean? That had to have been Kassia . . . so was delaying the handover of the elixir just more of her plan?

Jed rubbed at his wrist as Carter unlocked the chain from the arm of the chair. He gestured to Victor. Jed presumed they were going to reattach the second cuff Victor held. Instead, Victor nodded and slipped the cuff around his own wrist.

Jed groaned. Was he to be locked to Victor like a criminal? But Carter did not reach for the restraint and reattach it. The golden chain from Jed's cuff hung free.

'You will lead us to the elixir, Fulcanelli,' Montgomery confirmed.

'What's with the handcuffs?' Jed demanded, pointing at Victor's wrist.

'Science and alchemy,' scoffed Montgomery. 'Such nervous partners in the past. You know, of course, that alchemists long ago were hung for their crimes. And yet today modern scientists grapple with exactly the same issues and dilemmas that faced those alchemists of old.'

This answer wasn't making sense. It didn't explain why Victor was wearing a restraint just like Jed's own. Suddenly a blue light on Jed's cuff began to glow. He looked up. There was a glowing blue light on Victor's cuff too.

'Most of us are returning now to The Shard,' continued Montgomery. 'We have systems in place that we need to activate. Machinery set ready to replicate the elixir once you have brought it to us. Victor shall be your companion. You will do well not to try and escape from him.'

Were these people totally stupid? Didn't they realise that the handcuffs had to be attached to each other in order to keep him and Victor together? He'd just run away – he'd certainly proved he could do that time and time again.

Carter was enjoying his confusion. 'You are thinking about the golden chain?' he teased. 'Oh, Fulcanelli, science has made advances even if as yet we are behind you in our race for eternal life.'

The blue light on Jed's handcuff glowed brighter. He could just make out a gentle humming noise.

'The restraints are attached,' said Carter. 'Though not in the way you suppose.'

Victor held out his arm and Jed could see that the light on his cuff was glowing more brightly too.

'If you are ever out of Victor's range,' added Montgomery, 'a button will automatically detonate.'

Victor rotated his wrist to show a tiny raised point on his cuff that looked more like the head of a screw.

'When detonated, the cuff will send a surge of electricity through you.'

'You want to try and kill me?' Jed blurted. 'Haven't you proved you can't do that?'

Montgomery's voice was clipped in answer. 'We may not be able to kill you, Fulcanelli. But there are worse things than death. We can cause you pain.'

Jed shrugged dismissively. How could they hurt him? After everything he'd been through?

Montgomery's smile widened. Jed could tell the man was toying with him.

Montgomery led his way towards the back of the room, grabbed Kassia from her seat and dragged her towards where Jed was seated. 'The cuff you wear, Fulcanelli, has a twin.'

Carter seized Kassia's arm and pulled it flat so that Jed could see the circle of metal, tight around her wrist. A light glowed blue.

'All you feel, she will feel,' leered Carter, snapping the chewing gum between his lips. 'Do you understand?'

The horror of Jed's understanding was overwhelming. Could he let Kassia be hurt even if she'd betrayed him?

As if to answer Jed's question, Carter plunged down the button on Victor's wrist.

The lights on Jed and Kassia's cuffs burned red. Sparks flew upwards. Shock catapulted through every fibre in Jed's body, slinging him to the floor. As he looked up, he saw Kassia writhing on the ground beside him.

'Stop it!' he screamed. 'Stop it now!' It didn't matter what she'd done. It didn't matter how she felt about him. He knew that now. For him, nothing had changed. And even though he realised that what he said next would end it all, for ever, Jed blurted over her sobs, 'She has the elixir. It's in her pocket.'

Carter released the button and Kassia curled into a ball, sobbing and clutching at her wrist. Montgomery grabbed Kassia's shoulders and twisted her round to face him. Then he plunged his hands into her coat pockets.

'It's inside the case of a watch,' Jed mumbled, his words suffocating at the thought of what would happen when Montgomery found it.

Montgomery withdrew his hands. A small plastic disc fell to the floor and rolled between them. But no watch. Apart from the disc, Kassia's pockets were empty.

Two realisations hit Jed firmly between the eyes and he bent forward slightly as if the blows had been tangible. Kassia had hidden the elixir so it must still be safe. But somehow, more important than that, the disc that lay on the floor between them looked like some sort of tracking device.

Jed's mind catapulted him back to the chase through the streets to Little Venice. And to where Victor had grabbed Kassia as she'd tried to clamber over the wall to escape him. Kassia *had* led NOAH to the sea fort. But she had done so without knowing.

Jed felt air gush into his lungs, though the relief he felt was short-lived.

The light on the cuff sparked red again and current coursed through Jed's arm. He fell, clutching wildly at his wrist. Blood oozed from the cut in his life-line on to the pulsating band of metal.

Kassia squirmed and crumpled, thrashing around on the floor.

'You offer us untruths, Fulcanelli,' spat Montgomery. 'We need no lie detector to show us that.'

Jed cried out as the energy pummelled through his body. Kassia struggled beside him. And Montgomery laughed until the light on the cuffs turned back to blue.

Finally, Montgomery raised his cane. 'Let us tell you how this little game will play out,' he said, motioning towards the minders who took Jed by either arm and led him through the double doors of the chamber. Victor and Carter followed. Jed could tell that Kassia was being dragged after them. He could hear her sobbing.

'Please don't hurt her,' he yelled, struggling to turn.

'Whether she gets hurt or not is now in your control,' Montgomery hissed.

They made their way through the network of tunnels and passageways, up stairs and through corridors. And suddenly they were outside in the light of the day and on the busy streets of London. Buses raced past. Taxis blared their horns and gaggles of tourists angled selfie sticks skywards, jostling for the best position outside the famous building.

'Now, remember,' said Montgomery, hissing again into Jed's ear. 'Don't make a scene. Unless you want your friend to thrash around again in agony.'

Jed gritted his teeth.

They walked for a while, following the lead of

Martha Quinn, until they reached the end of the building and the huge tower that drove up towards the sky.

'Big Ben?' blurted Jed. 'You've brought me to Big Ben?' He could see from the clock face high above him that it was nearly ten.

Montgomery shook his head. 'Details, details, Fulcanelli,' he groaned. 'The devil is in the detail.'

Jed had no idea what he was on about. Weren't he and Victor supposed to be going to St Paul's?

'The tower is called the Queen Elizabeth Tower,' pressed on Montgomery. 'It is the bell inside that bears the name Big Ben.'

This little history lesson wasn't helping. Jed was trying to do calculations in his head. Fourteen. There were fourteen hours left.

'But it's not the bell or in fact the tower we are interested in,' cut in Montgomery. 'It is the clock you need to concern yourself with.'

If only the man had any idea how true that was.

Jed glanced behind him to try and see Kassia. She was clutching at her arm, her shoulders bowed, her legs looked as if they were about to buckle.

'You tried to make us believe that you had hidden the elixir in a watch,' said Montgomery. 'And for a moment I almost believed your little story. It seems we are not the only ones to know the legend about keeping the elixir inside a timepiece to strengthen its effects and power.' He pointed up at the enormous clock face that topped the tower, and looked out across the Thames. 'So let us use legend to guide us in our trade for the elixir,' he said.

Jed looked at Kassia again. She was doubled over, her hand clutched around her sides as if she was about to be sick.

'You know how we will monitor your progress, Fulcanelli. And we are even prepared to give you the time you need to complete our task. When you have safely retrieved that which we have spent so long looking for, you need to bring the elixir here, back to Queen Elizabeth's Tower. Then we can make a trade.'

'Trade for what?' Jed spluttered.

Montgomery stepped past the guard and forced open the door at the base of the tower and the minders who had accompanied Jed moved behind him, grabbing Kassia and dragging her between them towards the door.

'Trade for her,' sneered Montgomery.

The minders hauled Kassia inside and the door slammed shut.

'No!' Jed yelled, staggering forward. 'Let her go!'

The guard barred his access. The crowd thinned,

and even Carter and Martha Quinn drifted away, leaving only Victor and Montgomery.

'So you know the rules, Fulcanelli,' confirmed Montgomery. 'We will be at The Shard getting the machinery in place to make our dreams a reality at last. Your job is to fetch the means of making that dream tangible and bring it here. Create a scene or try to get away and Victor will activate the power surge.'

'And if I bring you the elixir?'

'We will do what we need to, to make eternal life an option for all who can pay.'

'And me? And Kassia? You'll let us go?'

Montgomery leant heavily on his walking cane. 'We are not unreasonable people,' he said, but Jed wasn't sure if this was the answer to his question. 'Let's start by saying you have until midnight, Fulcanelli.'

Jed knew as the words were uttered that the deadline NOAH had given him was the one that had already been set.

Cars raced past them. The air was thick with fumes. The pavement lined with people hurrying in all directions, heads down, splashing in puddles as they strode onwards. Some passed by talking to themselves loudly, headsets connected to phones hidden in their pockets. Others carried paper cups of coffee, sipping from them as they walked. Some raised cameras, standing so close to the edge of the road that the traffic grazed them as they set up the perfect Instagram shot. Winter coats, highly buttoned; scarves and gloves; umbrellas; shopping bags and little dogs. Jed clutched his hands to his head. It was too much. There were fourteen hours left to take the elixir. The elixir was missing. And Kassia was in trouble.

The world was pressing in on him and he was sure he was going to drown.

When he moved his hands from his head he saw they were shaking. And something else.

The fingers looked thinner than before. The skin seemed paler, almost transparent so that he could see suggestions of the bones below. His hand was fading. Or being erased.

'What time is it?' he barked.

Victor faced him awkwardly. 'February 27th.'

'I know what the date is!' Jed growled. 'I said what time?'

'Nearly eleven,' snapped Victor defensively. 'Why?'

Jed rubbed his hands but the colour did not return. Just a smear of blood from his weeping life-line, puckered across his thumb. Less than fourteen hours then. Closer to thirteen. He couldn't make the words he needed to answer.

Ideas crashed and thundered inside his head, competing with the noise of the city around them. Tears burned behind his eyes. 'I don't know where the elixir is,' Jed implored, staggering slightly where he stood.

'The lie detector told us it was at St Paul's,' said Victor. 'So St Paul's is where we're going.'

'It's not there!' Jed yelled.

Victor stood tall, his hand raised so the glowing cuff around his arm was visible. 'I'm not interested in your deception any more. You lied! The machine showed that. Then you tried to trick us again, about the girl.'

'It's not at St Paul's,' Jed yelled again.

'Liar!' spat Victor. 'From the very first time we spoke to each other, you've dragged me into untruths time and again. And I cannot be lied to any more. By anyone. So we're going to St Paul's and we are ending this. Understand?'

Jed stumbled beside him, his mind racing. If he was to get Victor to believe him, he needed somehow to find a way of making this partnership NOAH had forced him into work. His mind ricocheted him back to the first time in the cage. When Jed had made Victor reach for the key and give him his freedom. It had been a mind game, then. He needed a mind game now.

'Who else has lied to you, Victor?'

The boy beside him faltered.

'NOAH? Montgomery? Carter? Someone else?'

Victor's eyes drew closer together. 'I've never known the truth completely. It's all been a mess. But I'm getting closer. St Paul's has held answers so far.'

What did Victor mean? St Paul's had held answers. And were the lies he'd heard connected to St Paul's? He tried to keep up, but the breath was catching in his lungs.

'It's all connected,' Victor said at last. 'St Paul's has always been important. And if you want to know about lies, then Reverend Cockren is holding stuff back, I know it.'

'Reverend Cockren?' Jed's brain was in overdrive. Wasn't that the name of the guy who'd found him as he'd clambered out of the river? The man who'd wanted Jed to leave the cathedral? How was he linked into all this chaos? Jed's thoughts swirled like water in a river, crashing against trees and branches that had blocked the route down to the sea.

'Victor, please. I need—'

'Don't talk to me about what you need,' Victor spluttered. '*I* need you to find the elixir.'

Jed looked down at his hand again. It flickered like a pixelating picture on a bad internet connection. The elixir was what he needed too. But how could they both have that?

Jed was suddenly aware of a black limo pulling alongside the kerb beside them. The back door opened. 'Get in,' Victor said.

Jed stumbled into the car and slid along the seat. Victor climbed in beside him and then he pulled the door closed. 'St Paul's Cathedral,' he said to the driver. 'Make sure you take the most direct route.'

The car pulled up outside the entrance to St Paul's. It was too cold for there to be many people sitting on the steps, but the forecourt was busy with people taking photos.

Jed and Victor climbed out of the car and the driver nodded and pulled silently away.

Jed looked up. The enormous dome of the cathedral strained upwards, tipped with a pointed tower and gallery. To the right of the central dome was a rectangular tower topped with an enormous clock face. The hands were drawing together. Marching towards midday.

Jed felt his knees quaking. He looked away from the clock face. His gaze was drawn to the left. A matching tower, with an empty round hole where maybe a second clock had been forgotten or removed.

Time was being stolen, minute by minute, and he was too muddled to know what to do. There were little more than twelve hours remaining.

'I don't know where to take you,' Jed cried.

Victor took a deep breath. Then he depressed the button on the glowing cuff that circled his wrist. Jed's knees gave way and he collapsed as electricity flooded every part of him. The image of Kassia squirming in agony hit him as sharply as the concrete steps crunched against his knees.

Victor hauled Jed to his feet. 'I have warned you there was no time for games, Fulcanelli. You are going to take me to the elixir. That's what NOAH demanded.'

But Jed knew the elixir wasn't at the cathedral. He'd hidden it in Kassia's coat and now he had no idea where it was! His hands flickered and twitched and he plunged them deep into his pockets. How could this ever come right?

Anger swelled up inside him. This whole situation was impossible.

'What's your deal, mate?' Jed hissed.

Victor dragged Jed towards the entrance to the cathedral and through the door into the nave. 'My *deal*?'

'This!' said Jed, pulling his hands from his pockets and flinging his arms wide not caring now if Victor noticed the flickering. 'This chasing and the hunting. What's in it for you? You want this everlasting life, do you?'

Victor steered Jed down the nave and towards seats at the centre of the cathedral. They were arranged in a circle under the enormous central dome. Then he forced Jed down into a chair and sat down beside him, turning so that his face was so close that he only needed to whisper. 'This isn't about me, River Boy. It's about you.'

Jed could see a vein pulsing in Victor's neck.

'But it *is* about you,' Jed said, without lowering his eyes. 'It's obvious why I'm involved. You? How old are you? Seventeen? Why are you tangled up with the search for immortality?'

Victor wriggled a little on his chair.

Then Jed remembered the cage. And he remembered how he'd persuaded Victor to give him the key. 'This is about your dad, isn't it?' he said.

Victor took a deep breath, then he turned on his chair so that he was facing the centre of the cathedral. He put his elbows on his knees and rested his face on the cup of his hands.

Jed said nothing. He knew that even though time was slipping away from him, he had to allow Victor to talk.

'You know he worked for NOAH,' Victor mumbled. 'He was looking for a way to live for ever. My mum and my sister were ill. Some sort of genetic thing. And all he wanted to do was save them.'

Jed held Victor's gaze, scared to break the mood. 'But he didn't?'

Victor shrugged. He let his shoulders fall. 'They both died and he could do nothing to help them. And then he lost his life too. And I don't know how or why.'

Jed sat in the silence. 'Maybe we're the same, then,' he said slowly. 'Me and your dad.'

Victor reared up, his hands slapping to his side. 'You are not the same!'

'Aren't we?' Jed tried to keep his voice steady. The trembling in his hands was quickening.

'You're going to live for ever!' Victor spat. 'And my dad's dead. How can you possibly be the same?'

Jed tried to fence away the anger. He wanted to scream that this wasn't true and that in less than twelve hours his life would be over, but he forced himself to focus. Forced himself to drive on with his argument. 'We wanted the same thing, your dad and I. A way of helping those we were scared of losing.'

Victor turned in his seat. Something registered behind his eyes and Jed was sure that, for the first time since they'd stared at each other through the bars of the cage in The Shard all those months ago, Victor was seeing him as something different than a thing to catch.

'When you let me out of the cage all that time ago,' said Jed, 'you did it because you knew I was just a boy.'

'I was wrong about that!' growled Victor. 'You are not just a boy!'

'But I am! With the same wants and hopes as you!'

Victor looked at the ceiling above them. Paintings looped around the spread of the dome. Jed had never looked properly at them before. He guessed they were scenes from the bible. And one seemed to be shining. The noon-day sunlight from the windows was being funnelled against one particular image, making it sharper and clearer than the rest.

'I would have liked to have known your dad,' Jed said quietly.

Victor reached into his pocket and pulled out a tiny tattered photograph. The edges were bent and feathered where the picture had been worn away by time.

'Here,' said Victor, and he passed the photograph over.

Jed took the image with hands that flickered and faded. The fingers, like the edges of the photograph, looked like they were being dissolved.

A swirl of thick black memory swelled behind Jed's eyes. It thickened and twisted, stretching to become the body of a dragon, which curled round and round, reaching for its tail. In the centre of the space carved out by the rotating dragon, an image began to form. The image flickered into fragmented pixels as if the electrical signal carrying the memory was ebbing and flowing.

Jed scrunched his eyes against the recollection. He didn't want to see it! It was the final memory. The one from the Dark Church. The memory that had driven Kassia away. The memory that had changed everything he'd seen before. *A church, far away, in a quiet village. Kassia's dad waiting, ready to hand over the elixir. Another man entering the church. A man from the hurricane day, swept in now, not on the side of NOAH any longer, but come to deliver a warning. Orin Sinclair. And another man. A vicar. There is noise and shouting and Orin is falling, his side caught against the wing of the statue of a golden eagle, the skin ripped and bleeding. And the vicar cradles the man in his arm as he lies dying.*

Jed pulled himself out of the memory. The dragon spun and thickened. Its body contracted and exploded into fragments of dust and sound.

Jed tipped himself off the chair and crashed to his

knees. 'I knew him,' he mumbled.

'You knew my dad?' Victor spluttered, moving down to kneel beside him. 'How? When?'

Jed pushed against the floor, the photograph creasing in his fingers. 'In France. Twice. He was injured and I helped him.'

'You helped him on the day he died?'

Jed gritted his teeth. 'No. Not on the day he died. The time before.'

Victor reached round and grabbed Jed's shoulders, manoeuvring his body so that he had to face him. 'You were there on the day he died. And you didn't help?'

Suddenly, there was a voice behind them. A flurry of concern. 'Can I help you both? If you would like me to offer prayers on your behalf then there is a prayer book where you can add your name.'

Two shiny shoes stopped in front of them. A long black cassock skirted the floor.

Victor looked up first and there was a jolt of recognition from the visitor. 'Victor?'

The Reverend knelt down and Jed lifted his face to see him. The dragon was back. Fragments of darkness spiralling in from the corner of Jed's mind, merging and melding to form a spinning body. In the space created and left blank, Jed's brain flung out a memory that flickered and pulsed into view. *The day of the river, soaked and stumbling out of the Thames. A man reaching to help him. Who are you? What is your name? Inside the confines of the cathedral. Kassia standing beside him. A hat to hide Jed's identity. The same man, his face crinkled in concern, ushering them from the building.* And then the dragon churned the air created to contain the memory and another image flashed as if projected on to a screen. *The village church, a vicar cradling a man who is just about to die.*

Jed recoiled as if he'd been burnt. The dragon pressed against his eyes, forcing only blackness to remain. It shattered into a thousand pieces and blew away on the air, trapped under the dome of the cathedral.

Jed looked up into the face of Reverend Cockren. 'You were there too,' he spluttered.

The Reverend dragged them both to their feet and ushered them towards the back of the cathedral, through a door and up a flight of stairs. He threw his office door open and steered them both inside.

Victor shook free of Reverend Cockren's grasp, lifting his hands in defiance. 'OK,' he yelled. 'This is all too weird and confusing. You two know each other! And you – ' he jabbed his finger at Jed, who staggered backwards – 'you knew my father too! You were there when he died! With him!'

'Please,' said Reverend Cockren.

'Don't you *please* me,' shouted Victor. 'How long have we been playing this game? A year? And no one has given me any straight answers.' He pulled up his sleeve and gestured towards the button on the glowing cuff. 'I think it's about time I finally got all the answers I want, don't you? Or his friend will suffer for your secrets. Am I making myself clear?'

'Tell him,' Jed pleaded. 'Tell us. How we are all connected.'

Reverend Cockren turned his back, reached across the desk, picked up the telephone and pressed the dial to make an internal call.

'What are you doing, old man?' yelled Victor.

Reverend Cockren ignored the outburst and spoke into the receiver. 'Activate a Level Three evacuation,' he said calmly. 'I want the cathedral cleared of all visitors and staff.'

There was some fairly loud muttering from the other end of the line.

'That's right,' Reverend Cockren said calmly. 'The whole building totally empty. No panic. And no press. Then lock the doors.'

The chaplain lowered the receiver and as the clock struck one behind him, he finally began to explain.

* * *

'I am a Brother of Heliopolis,' Reverend Cockren said calmly. He reached inside the neck of his dog collar and pulled out a thin golden chain. Hanging from it was the mark Jed knew so well. A circle inside a square inside a triangle. The Reverend let the medallion hang, glinting in the sun that streamed through the window. Then he let go and it bounced against his chest.

'You?' snarled Jed. 'You drove me out of the cathedral. You didn't want anything to do with River Boy.' He struggled to make sense of what the Reverend was saying. 'And now you're telling me that, after all this time, you were here to help me? The first person I met when I clambered out of the Thames?'

'I didn't know who you were!'

'But you worked it out. And you sent me away without helping.'

'Maybe you weren't ready. Maybe I knew from experience it was best to wait.'

'Experience,' snapped Jed.

'There were three Brothers of Heliopolis based in London,' Reverend Cockren continued nervously. 'Tristan Devaux was one.'

'Kassia's dad,' Jed confirmed.

'And then your father,' Reverend Cockren said, turning to face Victor.

'My dad worked for NOAH! What d'you mean he

was one of these Brothers of whatever?'

'The Brothers of Heliopolis work to try and keep Fulcanelli safe. And protect the elixir.'

'You're wrong!' Victor snapped. 'My dad wasn't *helping* the unicorn. He was *hunting* him. And he can't have had the elixir. That's impossible. If he'd known about that, then . . .'

Reverend Cockren took his medallion and tucked it out of sight.

Victor hadn't finished. 'The letter you wrote me. The stuff you showed me. It was all about my dad and NOAH!'

'And your father's work began with NOAH,' Reverend Cockren said.

'So you've been lying to me!' Victor's face was buckling with rage.

'No. Not lying. Being selective. He *did* work for NOAH. Though he began to understand that things were not quite as simple or as one sided as the people he worked for made them out to be.'

'He changed sides?' groaned Victor.

'Yes.'

Victor said nothing and Jed saw his chance for answers too. 'On the night in my memory, the three of you are in Paris. And I ran and . . .' The words caught in his throat.

'You ran because NOAH had caught up with us. And our task as Brothers was never completed.'

'Hold on! Hold on!' yelped Victor, obviously still processing the earlier parts of the conversation. 'You said you were protecting the elixir? But my dad can't have had it. And he's dead. And the girl's dad is dead, isn't he? So does that mean that you—'

'Had the final elixir? Yes.'

'Final?'

'A sixth bottle,' Reverend Cockren explained. 'And for years I protected the elixir here at St Paul's. But we all knew . . . the three of us from that church in the village . . . we knew that Fulcanelli needed more than the elixir. He needed answers.'

Victor batted this away. 'I'm not interested in answers. Where is the elixir?'

'Not interested in answers?' said Reverend Cockren. 'I thought they were *all* you wanted.'

'But *you* said the elixir is here. *He* said it was here.' Victor waved his hand towards Jed. 'What can be more important than the elixir? Whatever side my dad was on, that was what he wanted, surely!'

'It's not here any more,' Jed spluttered. 'I tried to tell you. It was, but it's gone. We found where it had been hidden and we took it with us.'

Victor spun round and the Reverend's eyes widened.

'Well, like I said,' said Reverend Cockren calmly. 'The elixir and the answers were guarded in the same way.'

'The phoenix man,' mumbled Jed.

'What is he on about now?' exclaimed Victor, banging his hands against his thighs.

'The phoenix man,' Jed said again. 'John Donne. He was the Dean of this church and a statue of him survived the Fire of London. And we found the elixir hidden underneath it.'

'Well, maybe John Donne has more to tell you,' Reverend Cockren said quietly. 'Maybe he hides more than the elixir.'

The Reverend turned and took down a book of poetry from the shelf.

'That book!' said Victor. 'The one you lent me. The one I didn't understand.'

Reverend Cockren nodded, leafing through the pages until he found the poem he was searching for and thrust it towards Jed. Jed recognised the title of the poem from the book Kassia had brought in the box to *The Voyager*. 'That night in France, Tristan Devaux had brought various books for you to see. But like the day you came out of the Thames, you weren't ready then to see what you needed to.'

Jed scanned the words. 'This poem is about death,'

he said, his fingers flickering as he held the book in his hand. He remembered that back on the narrowboat he had put the book down before reading the end of the poem. The volume was open on his bed when Kassia had woken him.

Jed read the poem now and the final line scored its way across his mind. *'And death shall be no more; death thou shalt die.'*

Jed felt a wave of strength flood through him. He knew with more certainty than he had known anything since being dragged to the Star Chamber that he needed to return to the statue of John Donne, even if the elixir now was missing.

'Where are you going?' yelled Victor, hovering his fingertip over the button on the cuff.

'To the statue of John Donne outside the cathedral,' Jed said.

Reverend Cockren walked in front of him and blocked his way. 'What was the message on the Emerald Tablet, Fulcanelli? After all your time in Turkey, what was the lesson you learnt?'

'What is above so it is below,' he said.

'Two places, then,' said Reverend Cockren. 'Outside and in.' He paused. 'There are two statues of John Donne. Why do you think I have emptied the cathedral? The answers you need, and the ones you are finally ready for, are at the other statue.'

Jed pushed past him and made for the door.

'What about the elixir?' bellowed Victor, poking his fingertip again in the direction of the button on the glowing cuff.

'You will not hurt her,' Jed said forcefully. 'You said that all you wanted were answers. Don't you owe it to your dad to let me find them?'

Jed heard the office clock chime two as they walked along the corridor and back towards the main part of cathedral.

Ten hours. He had only ten hours.

Every step across the tiled floor rang out, echoing against the vaulted ceiling. Jed noticed that prayer candles arranged on wire stands in the space beside the altar were no longer burning, their flames snuffed out. It was colder than before.

Reverend Cockren carried the poetry book in his hand and led the way past the circular space under the dome where Jed and Victor had been seated when he found them. He reached the inside line of aisle on the furthest side of the altar. Then he stopped.

'Here,' he said. 'The second statue.'

The wall of the cathedral curved away to the left, a tall, bowed window looking out on to the city. To the right, a towering, flat window. Light poured in. Between the two windows was an expanse of clean white stone wall. And in the centre of this, framed by an archway of dark black granite, was a long, thin and unassuming figure carved from marble.

The figure was of a man. He had the same beard and piercing eyes as the statue of John Donne that stood outside the cathedral. But this man seemed to be wearing some sort of crown. The whole of his body was wrapped in what looked like a bed sheet made of stone. He was standing on a small stone pot shaped like an urn. One of the handles of the urn was broken and there was a streak of lighter stone or discolouring around the base.

'What's so special about this?' said Victor, standing behind Jed.

'This is one of the most important statues in the cathedral,' said Reverend Cockren.

'Why?' went on Victor. 'Looks pretty ordinary to me.'

'This statue was in the first St Paul's,' said the Reverend. 'When the Great Fire of London hit the cathedral, and the lead from the roof melted and the floor gave way, this statue sank down into the crypt. It was the only thing to survive.'

'So this is the true phoenix man,' whispered Jed.

'Caught between two worlds. I don't understand. If the bottle of elixir was hidden below the statue outside, then what can be here?'

Reverend Cockren took a deep breath. 'The Brothers of Heliopolis charged me to keep the sixth elixir safe. And so, in 2012, when a new statue of Donne was put outside the cathedral, I made sure the elixir was stored below it. But long, long ago, before that, the answers you would really need, Fulcanelli, were guarded by *this* statue.'

'There's something under this statue too?' Jed asked.

'What if there is?' snapped Victor, obviously keen to interrupt what had become a private conversation. 'NOAH sent me here to get the elixir. What can this stone guy be hiding that is worth more?'

Reverend Cockren spun round. 'Haven't you been paying attention to *anything* I've been saying? Your father rejected what NOAH was looking for. Surely you trust that what he sought instead was more important!'

Victor frowned. 'I'm undecided,' he snapped. 'I don't know where we are with all this stuff about my father. So I guess you'd better get on and explain!'

Reverend Cockren shook his head. 'It doesn't work like that. I can't tell you the answers. That's called preaching!'

'Isn't that what you do?'

'Perhaps. Yes. But I like to think I just get people to ask questions.'

'Oh, I'm asking, all right!' thundered Victor.

Jed held up his hand, signalling for quiet. 'You say the real answer is here.'

Reverend Cockren nodded.

Jed stepped closer to the statue. He peered at the urn at John Donne's feet, his eyes drawn to the broken handle and the mark smeared across the surface. 'What is that?' he said, bending down, his eyes level with the discoloured section of the urn.

'A scorch mark from the fire,' said Reverend Cockren quietly.

Jed reached out his hand. He placed the tip of his fingers on the mark.

The bolt through his fingers was like electricity. For a second he thought Victor must have pressed the button on the cuff he wore, but the surge of power was more intense even than the one that Victor controlled. Jed's spine arched and he was lifted from his feet and catapulted backwards, flung upwards so that his body scythed through the air. He thudded to the ground, his back crunching against the floor, his head flung hard against the tiles.

Darkness pressed against his eyes. It thickened and

pulsated, stretching into the body of the dragon that had circled and protected every memory. This time the dragon wasn't spinning and swirling, carving a circle in the air. It reached upwards, extending into a line that speared forward like an arrow. The body of the dragon crashed against the pillar that faced the statue of John Donne. It exploded into light and it was as if every candle across the cathedral had been relit. Heat churned upwards and it was a while before Jed realised it was coming from him. His chest tightened and constricted and the dragon scar on his chest throbbed. Jed folded into the pain. He knew that, finally, the mark of the dragon, burnt on to his body, was complete.

Jed was aware of hands reaching to help him. Reverend Cockren and Victor scooping him up to sit on one of the wooden chairs.

'What happened?' yelled Victor. 'I didn't touch the restraint.'

'I know, I know,' Jed mumbled. 'That was all me.'

He pressed his hand against the base of the chair, checking that the seat would support him.

'What happened?' Victor asked again.

Jed didn't answer. He looked past Victor and Reverend Cockren to the pillar behind them.

The pillar was like all the others in the nave of the

cathedral. Fairly plain at the base, but topped with carvings of fruit and flowers.

Jed remembered how in Turkey, inside the Hagia Sophia, people had stood in front of a similar pillar, hoping for a miracle. He had laughed at them and their hope that there could be answers contained somehow inside the stone. But as he looked up at the pillar he knew the answers he needed were hidden there.

At the top, disguised by the sculptor, where on all others he had carved fruit and flowers, there was something else. A dragon. Small and unassuming, like the statue of John Donne. But there to see, if you really looked.

This dragon wasn't circling. This dragon wasn't straining or reaching for its tail. This dragon was stretched like the final dragon that had formed in Jed's mind only seconds before. It was pointing like an arrow across the cathedral to the wall on the other side.

Jed stared hard. Then he rolled the edge of his shirt up away from his chest.

Victor stepped back from him in horror.

The welts and scars were raised and red, the branding now finished. A dragon circling but straining beyond its tail, its head reaching forward in the same direction as the stone dragon which topped the pillar.

'What is that?' hissed Victor.

Jed lowered the edge of his shirt. 'I guess it's my final answer.'

He pushed himself up from the chair and grabbed the poetry book that Reverend Cockren had shown him when they'd been up in his office. It felt lighter in his hand. He held it against his chest and his skin no longer felt as if it was burning.

'What are you doing?' said Victor, still obviously reeling from the sight of the scars that Jed had shown him.

'It's OK,' Jed said, stumbling forward, his legs catching against the line of chairs. 'It's going to be all right.'

'You should sit,' said Reverend Cockren, his face white with concern. 'Take things easy.'

'No,' said Jed, clutching at the book he carried. 'There's no need.'

He looked down. His hands were still flickering, drifting in and out of focus. The fading had stretched along his wrist and under the metal restraint and towards his elbows. But this didn't make him feel uncomfortable.

He made his way across the nave of the cathedral towards the far wall that faced the pillar.

'Where are you going?' Victor pressed.

Jed didn't reply. Ideas and memories bounced inside his mind. Not encircled by the body of a dragon this time, but clear and sharp, as though he was watching the scenes for the very first time. *Bergier the old man in the nursing home in Paris, leaning forward and his eyes locking on Jed's own. 'It's you,' he said to Jed. 'It's you.' The mosaic on the wall in the Hagia Sophia in Istanbul. A phoenix man, hidden but about to rise. The emerald dagger in the Topkapi Palace. A dangerous dagger given away and then returned, having never been used.* Why these memories? Of all they'd been through and all they'd seen and all they'd done, why these? Then a final memory, older and dragged from somewhere deeper. *An old man standing in a gasworks in Paris. The same man as from the first memory. Bergier, but younger, his eyes bright. 'I have a warning,' Fulcanelli said to the old man in the memory.* And then the memory cracked and splintered like shards of detonated glass and faded away.

'Jed!' Victor was calling him from behind. But Jed kept walking. Right across the nave, to the place where the dragon on his chest and the dragon on the pillar had been pointing.

An enormous sculpted angel stood either side of two huge black-and-gold doors. There was golden writing above the frame. Strong and square text that ran from one side to the other. Jed stopped walking. He took a deep breath. Finally he turned.

'I was there, Victor,' he said loudly so that the space echoed. 'When your father died. And I know now that he was doing what he thought was best.'

Victor and Reverend Cockren hurried forward.

'He had rejected NOAH and all that the organisation stood for,' Jed continued.

'I keep telling you, you're wrong,' said Victor. 'He wanted the elixir.'

'No,' Jed said calmly. 'He wanted me to see what Kassia's dad had brought.' He held out the poetry book.

'Poetry?' scoffed Victor. 'He thought that was more important than something that could make you live for ever?'

Jed walked forward, the book still balanced in his hand. He stopped in front of them in the middle of the nave. It was three o'clock. There were nine hours left. Single figures only.

The walkways spanned out in four directions like a crossroads. It was clear now that there were two choices he could take in this moment. He could find the elixir and give it to NOAH and they would set Kassia free. But if he did that and he handed over the elixir then his own chance for eternal life would vanish. Or he could find the elixir and try to escape somehow. This would leave Kassia as NOAH's captive and ensure he remained a hunted person for every one of the days that he got to live for ever.

Whichever decision he made, he could do nothing without Victor on his side.

'I am begging you,' Jed said, fixing his gaze firmly on Victor. 'Nearly a year ago I was inside a cage and you had no idea who I was. And you let me free. So I'm asking you now, knowing all you do, that you let me go.'

Victor made a sound like a stifled laugh. 'Let you go! Why would I do that?' He gestured to the metal band around his wrist. 'Even if I did, if you step out of my sight then this thing works automatically. Do you want to hurt Kassia?'

That was the last thing Jed wanted. That was why he needed Victor to free him.

Victor slipped his sleeve down over the metal cuff. 'Where would you go, anyway?'

'To find the elixir.'

Victor made the laughing noise again. 'You keep telling me you don't know where it is!'

'I will find it,' Jed said desperately. 'You need to let me do this on my own.'

Victor rocked his head back. 'You're mad, Jed! Why would I?'

Jed stepped closer. He could feel his chance slipping away and he needed to grab it with both hands. 'Because you have never really been sure about capturing me, have you?' He hesitated but Victor did not interrupt. 'All the times I've escaped, I know that part of you has been cheering me on.'

Victor scrabbled at his sleeve again and dragged it upwards to reveal his tattoo. A unicorn in chains. The mark of NOAH he had volunteered for them to brand him with. 'I am on *their* side!' Victor spluttered, but the words seem to clog in his throat.

Jed shook his head. He got closer still. 'Look at the chain, Victor,' he said as gently as he could. 'Tying the unicorn down when it was born to be free. Look at the reality of that.' He waited again but still Victor said nothing. 'There is so much more for that unicorn and you are keeping it prisoner. You don't have to follow their lead.'

Victor turned his arm. He slid the sleeve down over the tattoo and hid it again below the fabric of his shirt.

'Let me go, Victor. Give me till nine and I will come back, I promise.'

'I let you go before,' snapped Victor.

Jed remembered the cage. 'It was the right thing to

do then. And it is the right thing to do now,' he said. 'If you bring Kassia here at nine, I promise I will have the elixir.' Jed had no idea if he could keep his promise. But he'd made his choice. The plan was all he had.

'I still don't see why I should let you go,' Victor said in a voice Jed supposed he was trying to make sound determined.

Jed had only one option left. 'Because you know it's what your dad would have done,' he said.

Victor looked beyond Jed to the black-and-gold gates behind him. Time stretched between them like an elastic band.

Tentatively, Victor reached out and took Jed's arm. He took a key from his pocket and he slipped it into the lock of the metal cuff Jed wore. There was a clicking noise and the cuff sprang open.

'You understand,' Victor said, withdrawing the cuff and snapping it closed inside his pocket. 'That I can still hurt Kassia.'

Jed felt a tightening in his throat as he rubbed his naked wrist with flickering fingers.

'If you are not back by nine o'clock, then she will feel pain like she has never felt before.'

Jed drank in the smell of the river. He pressed his hands against the wall he'd climbed over nearly a year ago to get to the cathedral. Light was filtering in between the clouds and reflecting off the water.

His mind was racing. He remembered the kerbside in Prague when there had been nine months left to the ultimate deadline. The sea fort when there had been nine days. Now there were nine hours. He barely had the strength or courage to keep walking. But he knew now what he had to do.

He tried to slow his breathing though his body fought against him. His arms were quivering. His fingers flickering like faulty lightbulbs. Time was running out.

He needed the elixir. And that meant he needed Kassia.

He flagged down a London cab and piled into the back seat, scrabbling in his pocket for money. 'I've only got five pounds,' he jabbered at the driver.

'Three quid on the clock already,' said the driver. 'Minimum charge this time of day, mate. Where you going?'

'Queen Elizabeth's Tower!'

'Oooh, aren't you the fancy one? Big Ben to tourists. That's gonna cost you more than a fiver.'

'So take me as close as you can,' begged Jed.

'OK, mate. But money in advance if you're strapped for cash. I don't want you doing a runner 'cos you're saving your dosh for dinner at the Red Lion.'

Jed counted out the coins from his pocket, and the driver pushed the car into gear and set off.

'It's still a good mile from here,' the driver said at last, sliding open the screen between him and the back seat so he could see Jed more clearly. 'You all right, son?' he said quietly, maybe noticing Jed's face for the first time.

''Course,' said Jed. 'Just was out on the town last night.'

'Say no more, sunshine. Say no more.' He winked, and slid the screen back into position. 'Mind how you go, then.'

Jed wobbled out of the cab. His legs did not feel like they belonged to him and he wavered for a moment, stumbling against the kerb. His feet splashed in the rain clogged gutter.

The taxi driver laughed. 'Must have been quite a morning, mate.'

The taxi driver didn't know the half of it.

Jed took a moment to get his bearings before he began to run. His pace was uneven and his arms flailed a little in his attempt to keep himself upright, but at least the clock tower he was making for was a clear and obvious point of destination. Time loomed in front of him, pulling him like a magnet.

He was wet with sweat and his breath came in short, sharp gasps by the time he reached the bottom of the tower. What air there was, though, pitched out of his lungs as soon as he saw the door.

A guard was still stationed in front of it.

Jed ran his fingers through his hair. Kassia was inside the tower. She knew where the elixir was. And now was his chance to find it. But the guard stood between him and the entrance and he did not look like the kind of guy you argued with.

Jed ducked down behind a newspaper stall as he tried to wrestle his thoughts together and work out what to do.

He'd been crouched down for a moment when suddenly he realised there was someone staring at him.

'Are you OK?'

Jed looked up.

The woman peered at him. 'Are you?'

Jed struggled to stand and darted round the other side of the woman so that she blocked him from the view of the guard. 'I'm fine,' he lied. 'You?'

'Sure,' she laughed. 'Nothing that finally having this baby wouldn't put right. You try walking round London carrying a load like this. Tube is worse. All that pushing and shoving. Not safe in my condition, even if London Transport gives you a badge.' She gestured to a Baby-on-Board pin fastened to her lapel and then at her rather large baby bump. 'Still, as long as you're all right.'

Jed nodded again. 'But there is something you could do to help me if you don't mind.'

'Oh, my baby, my baby. It's coming! It's coming!'

The pregnant woman was howling and clutching at her stomach.

'That's great,' hissed Jed. 'Keep going!'

'Oooh, my baby!' yelled the woman, even louder.

The guard in front of the tower looked over.

'I think the baby's coming right now!' yelled the woman. She glanced across at Jed who was back crouched behind the newspaper stall.

He winked. 'Brilliant,' he mouthed encouragingly.

The guard glanced from side to side, but no one else was paying attention. Sightseers drove towards the next photo opportunity on their tour. Workers leaving their offices early had their heads down, determined to ignore all distractions. Traffic ploughed on.

'Please,' yelled the woman. 'Help me! Please!'

The guard looked over his shoulder. He fidgeted from foot to foot and then unable to ignore the woman's wails any longer, he hurried across the road towards her.

Jed nodded his thanks and raced to the tower door. The woman was rubbing her tummy and talking to the guard, who had hailed down a taxi and was giving the driver instructions while he pushed a twenty-pound note into his hands.

Jed did not stay around long enough to see what happened when the woman changed the destination from the hospital to the shops in Oxford Street. As far as he was concerned, the plan had worked perfectly. It had taken Jed a while to persuade the woman he wasn't doing anything illegal. And that the guard could totally afford the taxi fare as he would make the claim on office expenses from a business that was based in the penthouse floor of The Shard.

Now the guard was distracted, it was time to get inside.

The door wasn't locked. Stage two of the operation complete then. All he had to do was get to Kassia and NOAH had told him they would keep her inside the clock room, so all there was to do was climb. And climb. And climb.

Finally, the stairwell opened out on to a corridor. And in the middle of the corridor was a door. Kassia must be behind it.

But in front of the door were two more guards.

Jed cursed under his breath and hid at the top of

the stairwell.

The guards were talking. Mumbled conversation. About the weather. And football scores.

Jed cursed again. How could he trick both of them into leaving? His hands were flickering and the climb had sapped him of the little energy he had left. He wasn't strong enough to take them on.

Suddenly, the conversation changed tack. Something about the girl being on her own and how she must be scared.

Relief rushed through him. If there were no guards *inside* the clock room then maybe there was another way to get to Kassia.

It was, Jed decided, a plan that was full of risk. He also knew, without seeing the face of the clock, that by now it must be nearly five. He didn't really have time to fill in a risk assessment and come up with a safer option. All he could think was that he was glad he'd had to do the abseiling in Turkey, even if that had involved descending into a pit and facing his greatest fear.

He had climbed two more flights of stairs and was now on a balcony that ran along the top of the Queen Elizabeth Tower. He was strapped to a rope-and-pulley system that he guessed was used by cleaners when they scaled down to clean the clock face.

He would have preferred to have taken a lift. At the very least, he would have preferred there to be someone feeding the rope out for him. But if abseiling was the only way to get to Kassia, then that was what he had to do.

Jed swung his leg over the lip of the wall and teased the rope through his fingers. He tried not to focus on the flicker and the fading. He tried not to think about how his legs wobbled and how he wasn't really far enough away from the clock face to use his legs to steady him. He tried not to think about how he was really just hanging there. He tried to focus on the time and the surface under his feet at least made that part of the mission possible.

The clock face was, as he'd hoped, smooth and shiny like frosted glass. As the sun had now nearly set, a light inside the tower was making the whole clock face glow. Annoyingly, the face wasn't totally transparent, but it was clear enough for him to see through to the clock workings beyond. And to Kassia.

She was framed inside the gap made by the hands of the clock. Half past five. Six and a half hours remained.

Kassia flung herself forward, her hands outstretched. He could see that she was speaking, though the glass was too thick to allow sound to get through.

But that didn't matter.

Jed could still speak to her. And she could speak back. If they used sign.

'Are you mad?' Kassia signed, her words enormous and loud despite their silence. 'Someone will see you!'

'If they do, they'll just think I'm cleaning,' Jed signed back. 'People will see what they want to see. Like they do in memories.'

Her fingers stuttered a little, and he regretted his words, but then she was signing again, frantically now, against the glass. 'I didn't tell them!'

'I know. I know.' He signed slowly. 'They put a tracker on you. That's how they knew.'

She moved away a little, her silhouette blurring and buckling in the light.

'Have they hurt you?' he signed.

He could see her shake her head, a shadowy shape behind the glass.

'I don't have long,' Jed signed.

He could see her frustration as she threw her hands up. 'Just over six hours,' she signed.

Jed wobbled a little on the rope. He glanced at the road below him and the river raced past and he felt his stomach falling like it had somehow escaped his body. 'You need to tell me where the elixir is,' he signed.

There was a pause. Her hands were still behind the glass.

'Kassia?'

'I gave it to Dante.'

Jed's stomach fell again and this time it wasn't because he'd looked down. The elixir was in Herne Bay. That was miles away. So it was over then. The race was finished. He had failed.

Suddenly, he heard a rapping on the glass.

'He will have got back to London,' Kassia signed. 'I know he will!'

'But where will he be? And where will he have put the elixir?'

Kassia's answer was jagged and faltering. 'I think he will take it to where I go when I can't cope.'

'You need to be sure,' Jed said. He couldn't waste a moment by following the wrong lead.

'I know he will,' signed Kassia.

Jed thought back to Spain and how Dante had tracked him down when he had thought his world was over.

'Not Fleet Street?' Jed signed. 'Not Postman's Park?'

'No,' Kassia signed more securely. 'He will take it to the graveyard. He will leave it with our dad.'

Jed hung for a moment and the rope swung a little

in the wind. He tugged himself closer to the window and he made his signs as large as he could against the window. 'Kassia. When you said you were angry . . .'

'I *am* angry, Jed!'

He wobbled again on the rope. His hands flickered and pulsed.

'But not at you any more! I'm angry with *time*!' She thumped her hand, palm outstretched, against the glass.

Jed pressed his palm against hers, the clock face a barrier between them. It felt as if they were touching. Connected.

He pulled his hand away reluctantly. 'Do you trust me?' he signed slowly.

'How many times do you have to ask that?'

'Just once more,' he signed.

She made one word only with her fingers. 'Always.'

'So you must do exactly what NOAH asks of you. Understand?'

Both of her hands were against the glass now. 'Jed, promise me you'll get the elixir.'

His answer was simple. 'I promise.' He pressed his hand against hers again. It left a smear of blood as he pulled away.

And then he began his ascent back up to the balcony.

* * *

The clock at the newsagents beside the entrance to the cemetery said it was seven o'clock. Two hours left to get back to the cathedral. Five hours left before . . .

Jed walked alone down the central avenue to the grave.

He was exhausted, every muscle in his body crying out for him to stop. With no money left, he'd been forced to run across the city. The thought of running back again was overwhelming. And he could only return if what he looked for was actually here.

There was no one else in the graveyard. The gates had been locked and he'd had to climb over them. It seemed ironic he'd had to fight his way in to be with the dead.

The moon cast her light across the headstones. Some memorials were newly decorated with flowers. At others, there were no flowers at all, not even a vase. This made him sad.

He hurried towards the back of the cemetery. The graves here were newer.

Jed remembered the first time he'd come. Kassia had brought him shortly after they'd first met. And he remembered the last time he'd come here too. Then, he'd been on his own and he had carried an orange rose. This time he carried nothing. He hadn't come to leave a message. He'd come to collect.

Tristan's grave was in the shadow of a huge evergreen tree, set apart a little from the other graves. The tree cut up the light of the moon so it fell in pieces, dappling the ground.

Jed felt the normal knotting inside him when he saw the date written across the headstone. The fifth elixir day. The date that had begun some of his remembering. A day that had changed everybody's life in the Devaux family, before Jed had even clambered out of the Thames and thrown everything further into chaos. He knew now, as he hadn't done then, that the man buried here had been sent to help him. Had come with another solution which had seemed so muddled when he'd shared it.

Jed's knees weakened a little and he lowered himself to kneel.

The flowers in the vase looked fresh and he wondered if Anna had brought them. Or if, as he hoped, Dante had been here.

The flowers were purple. Jed remembered what the colour meant. *Hope for the impossible.*

Jed ran his hands across the grass, pressing his fingers against the thin border that edged the stone. The grass was longer here, obviously not trimmed since the last days of summer.

There was nothing hidden, though. No openings in the ground like there had been under the statue of John Donne. There was only the vase of purple flowers, coloured to signify something that might not happen.

Maybe Dante hadn't been, after all. Maybe what seemed obvious to Kassia hadn't been obvious to her brother. Maybe he had chosen another place. Or maybe he had no intention of passing the elixir on.

Jed clenched his hands and pulled them towards his face. His arm shuddered, the fingers now so pixelated and faded that they were hard to move in the way he wanted to. His arm brushed against the vase and it toppled forward. Water cried on to the grave and the petals on some of the blooms creased and tore.

Jed fumbled to return the flowers to the vase. And moonlight from between the branches of the tree flashed on metal.

He clutched the flowers to him, laying them across his palm. And there, tied to the stem by a thin silver chain, was the pocket watch.

Jed worked it free of the flowers. He rubbed the engraved swallow with the heel of his thumb and he clicked the case open.

There were no workings now. Time had stopped and the hollow space contained just one thing. The bottle of elixir.

Jed eased it out of the watch case. He held it up to the light and the golden liquid inside swirled and churned.

The branding on Jed's chest smarted and tightened.

Jed covered the elixir with his hand. Blood from the open life-line ran down the edge of the bottle and for a moment Jed closed his eyes.

The answer was here. If he uncorked the bottle and drank, everything he had ever feared would be over. Life stretching on and on so that this place and a grave like this one would never be a reality for him.

But Jed did not break open the seal.

He pushed the bottle back into the watch casing and shoved it in his pocket.

He had less than five hours until midnight. There was one thing left to do. And it was going to take all his remaining energy.

Kassia stumbled up the steps to the cathedral. Martha Quinn hung on to one arm and Carter the other, and she found it hard to keep pace with them.

Someone stood at the West Door, holding it open. She recognised him. The man who'd let her use the St Paul's library for her homework. The place where she'd worked out exactly who Jed was. Why was Reverend Cockren here? Carter had said that the cathedral would be closed and that Jed had asked that they all come and meet together. So where was Jed? Had he found the elixir?

'Come on, come on,' said Reverend Cockren. 'Let's get you lot inside. We don't want the general public wandering in. I've had to cancel evensong to ensure we had the cathedral to ourselves.'

Montgomery's walking cane made a clicking noise as he climbed the steps. 'I don't think irritations like that will matter when Fulcanelli has delivered what he promised,' he said.

The Reverend didn't answer as Kassia stepped past him and into the cathedral.

It was eerily quiet. Last time she had been in the main building, it had been busy with sightseers and pilgrims. But now, as the time approached nine o'clock, the space was empty.

The group stopped beside the font in the doorway. Kassia could see the water inside the deep stone container. It was still and unbroken by ripples.

'Jed? Where's Jed?' she blurted. She had no idea if he'd managed to find the elixir. But she knew with a certainty that pressed down, making it difficult to breathe, that there were only three hours left until midnight.

Carter squeezed her arm sharply and the metal cuff

she still wore around her wrist caught on the edging of his long leather coat. 'All in good time,' he said.

But Kassia knew they had no time! In only three hours, the full year since Jed had climbed out of the Thames would be over. These people still didn't know that he needed to take another dose.

Suddenly, Kassia saw two figures walking down the central aisle. Jed and Victor. She could see the metal bands still fastened around their wrists. Three parts of a chain that linked them together.

'Jed!' Kassia sobbed.

Carter tugged her arm even harder to make her silent.

'You have the elixir?' demanded Montgomery.

Jed nodded.

Kassia felt her pulse thunder inside her.

Montgomery bristled with expectation. 'So where is it?'

'Somewhere safe.'

Montgomery jabbed the flagstones with the end of his cane. 'I've had enough of your games, Fulcanelli.'

Jed thrust his hand forward and pointed at the manacle around his wrist. 'Don't talk to me about games!' he spat.

'Now, now. There's no need for annoyance. You changed the rules and demanded we came here to claim the elixir. I suggest you hand it over.'

Kassia scanned Jed's face for some clue to what he was doing. She couldn't work out the meaning of what she saw.

'The elixir is at the very top of this building,' Jed said.

Montgomery shot a look of annoyance in Victor's direction. 'You,' he growled. 'You were sent to make sense of all this.'

'I did,' said Victor quietly.

'And yet you tell me the elixir is still hidden?' The venom this time was aimed squarely at Jed.

'Not hidden. Just not down here at the moment. It will take me less than two hours to retrieve it.'

'So go on then!' yelled Montgomery, his voice echoing against the vaulted ceiling. He shook his shoulders, clearly trying to force himself to stay composed. He took a deep breath. 'We have waited decades. Two hours more will not hurt us.' He stepped so close that Jed had to turn his face away. 'But remember we have the means to hurt you, River Boy.' He snapped his head in Victor's direction, all reasonableness ebbing away. 'Maybe give them a reminder.'

'Sir, I don't know if—' Victor stumbled over his words.

Montgomery reached for Victor's wrist and pressed his finger down hard on the button.

Kassia's knees gave way as the electricity jolted through her.

She could hear Jed shouting though the pain was too great to be able to make out what he said. She tried not to cry, but she failed.

'You need to let her come with me,' demanded Jed, his words clear at last, as the pain throbbed its way out of her body.

'Don't be ridiculous!' snapped Martha Quinn, dragging Kassia from the ground so she stood awkwardly beside her.

Jed raised his hand. 'It wasn't a mistake that I found Kassia when I climbed out of the water a year ago. I need her to help me now.'

'Help you how?'

'I can't get the elixir alone,' Jed said.

'So go with Victor and bring it back to us,' cut in Carter, who was clearly losing patience.

'I *will* go with Victor. But if you want the elixir, Kassia has to come too.'

Montgomery turned to Martha Quinn and she mumbled something Kassia couldn't quite hear.

'Where could I escape to?' said Jed, opening his hands, which Kassia saw were flickering and twitching.

'Victor has the restraints. You know that I will never do anything to hurt Kassia.' Jed spoke as if they were the only two people in the great space of the cathedral, and Kassia so wanted it to be true.

'Let me go,' she babbled. 'Let me help him.' She knew this was what she would do. If the elixir was high up in the cathedral like Jed claimed it was, then whatever Victor did to her, she would make Jed drink it.

Montgomery spoke in hushed whispers. 'OK,' he said at last. 'You have two hours. Not a second more.'

'I won't need more,' Jed said.

Martha Quinn and Carter let go of Kassia's arms and she lurched towards Jed. He drew her into a hug. 'Do exactly as I say,' he whispered into her hair.

She nodded.

Victor led them back down the aisle towards the entrance to the stairwell leading up to the galleries. Kassia walked so close to Jed that their arms brushed together. 'Why are we—'

Jed cut her off. 'They're watching,' he said. He raised his finger to his lips and made a gentle shushing noise.

The flickering from his fingers was even more obvious now. 'Your hands. What—'

Jed made the shushing noise again and they kept walking.

As soon as they were inside the entrance to the stairs and out of sight of those who waited beside the font, Jed spun round to face Victor. 'You have to let us—'

'Hold on,' interrupted Victor. 'I don't have to do anything. No more favours, Jed.'

'Just one more,' Jed begged.

'He let you go earlier?' gasped Kassia. 'I thought somehow that you had—'

'You went to see her?' Victor interrupted again. 'I thought—'

Jed raised his hands to stop them both talking. 'Look, you, more than anyone, know we have little time to play with, Kassia. And you, more than anyone, know I have to keep NOAH on side, Victor. So I'm asking that you help us one more time. There are no exits from these gallery steps. We can't escape. And you can still hurt Kassia if I let you down.'

Kassia clutched defensively at her wrist.

Victor sighed. 'Oh, I don't know, Jed.'

'Please, Victor,' Jed said. 'For your dad.'

Victor took Jed's wrist and unlocked the restraint. 'They are timing you,' he said as he took the cuff and pushed it into his pocket.

'We are well used to racing the clock,' Jed said. He grabbed Kassia's hand and began to lead her up the stairs.

There were two hundred and fifty-seven steps and by the time Kassia had reached the top, she could hardly breathe and a stitch was digging into her side. 'Why have you brought me here?' she said.

Jed led the way through the doorway on to the Whispering Gallery. It circled round from either side of the door, a wide, open space above the floor of the cathedral and set inside the curve of the dome. There were raised stone steps running around the outside edge of the gallery against the wall, and a high metal fencing on the inside to stop people falling into the nave.

'This place is amazing,' Jed said brightly.

Kassia was confused. It was like he was a tour guide proudly showing off an excellent place to visit. 'Jed! The elixir!'

'It's up even higher than this gallery,' he said. 'But I wanted you to see this to understand how it works.'

'Works?' she said. 'What are you talking about? You haven't taken the elixir. You've got less than three hours left! Please, Jed, stop playing games.'

'This isn't a game, Kass. I am deadly serious.' He steered her to sit on the stone steps with her back against the wall. 'We will get the elixir in a moment. There are things I want to say first.' He turned and began to walk away from her around the edge of the gallery.

'Where are you going?' she cried, pushing her hands down to stand.

He raced back towards her and eased her into her seat again. 'Lean your head against the wall,' he said. 'It's called the Whispering Gallery because if I speak from the other side, the sound will carry straight to you and you'll be able to hear everything perfectly. It has something to do with sound moving at an angle and bouncing off the wall. Triangles carry the noise. You have to concentrate and give it all your focus otherwise the words will distort.'

'Jed, please. I don't want you to—'

'I need to, Kass. Let me do this one thing. And then we will go and get the elixir.'

'OK.' It made no sense. But then, had any of the things they'd done throughout the year made sense? If Jed needed her to listen, she would.

Jed walked halfway around the inner rim of the gallery and then he sat down. He looked across the space between them and then he leant his own head back against the wall and began to speak.

And carried somehow through the fabric of the walls, Kassia heard every word.

'I have learnt so much from my time with you,' he

said gently, and it was as if he was whispering directly in her ear. 'From Dante too. And the silence. And the signs. All the different ways of sharing. And I wanted to say thank you.'

Kassia turned her own head and breathed her answer into the wall. It was impossible to tell if he heard her. 'Jed, you're scaring me. Why can't we just go and get the elixir and you take it? You said when we were in the sea fort that perhaps you had to take it on the day the year was up. We're nearly there, Jed. The time has come. You need to take the elixir and escape.'

His answer came back through the wall. 'They will hurt you if I leave.'

She rubbed the cuff on her wrist. 'But they can't hurt *you*. And you will be free.'

She pressed her ear to the wall. The answer took so long to come she was afraid there wouldn't be one. 'Neither of those things are true,' he said.

'I don't understand.'

'Living for ever,' he said, and the whisper was so faint she had to strain her ears to hear. 'Wouldn't that hurt other people?'

Kassia reared away from the wall. Not this argument again. But separated from the wall she knew he would not hear her words and so she pressed her cheek against the cold stone and she began to argue. 'You can't think about the other elixir days and the disasters.'

'I'm not talking about disasters,' he said. 'I'm talking about every day afterwards. Isn't the fact that our time here is rationed a good thing? Imagine what it would be like to be stuck. Frozen in time. Alone.'

'You wouldn't be alone,' she pleaded.

'So you'd take the elixir too, if we could find the recipe and make more? But where would we find it? We've spent a year searching. And what about Dante? Your mum? Nat? Giseppi? Amelie? How many people would we include if we made more?'

Kassia banged her hand against the wall and across the gallery she saw Jed recoil as if the noise had hurt him. 'I don't care about any of those things! I just want you to live for ever!'

His answer was so faint she wasn't sure she really heard it. 'I will,' he said.

They sat for a moment, their backs against the wall and the whispers silent between them.

'Can you see the paintings on the dome of the cathedral?' Jed asked at last.

Kassia peered forward and then returned to the wall. 'What about them?'

'One of the pictures is of this guy called Elymas,' said Jed. 'He was a sorcerer and the stories explain that he was blinded by his magic.'

'So? What has that got to do with us? With you?'

'It's just we have to be careful to see everything,' said Jed. 'To see what is really important. To not get blinded.'

Kassia pressed her hand against the wall. What she needed to say faltered in her mouth. She wanted to sign but Jed was too far away to read her words. 'You're scaring me, Jed.'

'Life is scary, Kass. Maybe being human is about being brave and facing that.'

She had no idea how to answer him.

A voice jolted her away from the wall. Montgomery was standing in the nave of the cathedral, looking up at the gallery. 'It's ten o'clock,' he shouted. 'Your time is running out, Fulcanelli.'

This truth of this statement snuffed out Kassia's breath.

When she leant back, Jed was once again beside her. 'Let's keep climbing,' he said.

They climbed for at least another hundred steps. Kassia clung to Jed's arm and they steadied each other as they got closer to the top.

'Dante hid the elixir all the way up here?' asked Kassia.

'No,' said Jed. 'It was where you said it would be. I just relocated it.'

'Why?' groaned Kassia.

'Because there were things I needed you to hear,' he said. 'And things I needed you to see.'

'You're making everything sound so final.'

Jed shook his head. 'Not final,' he said.

'I need you to promise me that—'

'I'm going to live for ever, Kass.'

She was quiet then, saving her breath for the climb.

When they reached the doorway this time, it led not to an inside gallery, but to a large, stone balcony that ran around the outside of the building. Stone balustrades, stretched up from the ground. They were as high as a man and to see the view Kassia had to press her face close to the gaps in the stone.

'Look,' said Jed, pointing his arm through the gap. 'Somerset House. Do you see it?'

Kassia peered in the direction he was pointing. 'I see it. What's it got to do with the elixir?'

'Everything,' he said, pulling her away from the balustrade and holding her hands. 'Promise me that you will go back there and skate. That you'll eat bags full of toffee and drink hot chocolate in the street.'

'*We'll* go back there and do those things!' she snapped.

'I will be with you,' he said.

She tried to search his face for some clue about

what he was thinking. His eyes darted backwards and forwards, searching her own face and checking if she understood. But she didn't understand!

'Is this a trick?' she said at last. 'Is the elixir even up here?'

'Not here,' said Jed.

She pulled away.

'I mean not in this gallery. But hasn't everything always worked in threes? The three colours of the stages of alchemy? The triangle, the circle and the square. Even you, me and Dante.'

She didn't see what he was getting at.

'The elixir was always going to be in the third gallery, Kassia.'

'Why?'

'Because I couldn't leave it here. Not on a gallery made of stone. Because think of all those stone stories we tried to make sense of and how muddled we got. And I couldn't leave it below in the Whispering Gallery where speech can sometimes be distorted.'

'So what's the third gallery?' demanded Kassia.

'It's called the Golden Gallery.' Jed pulled in a deep breath of satisfaction. 'Gold and eternal life were the ultimate aim of the alchemists, weren't they? There was nowhere else I could put it.'

She nodded.

'Are you ready to climb?' He reached out once more and took hold of her hand.

'I'm ready,' she said.

Stone steps gave way to a spiralling metal staircase. It looked to Kassia like a fire escape, but as they rose she had the feeling that somehow they were climbing towards a fire and not away from one.

Finally, the stairs led to a series of stone archways. It felt almost as if they were underground in some ancient cave system. Then the space opened up and they stepped outside on to the Golden Gallery.

This balcony was smaller than the others. A metal handrail hemmed them in, but it was possible to see for miles across London, illuminated in the silver lights of night. For a moment Kassia forgot why she was here and gazed outwards. She could see the Houses of Parliament sparkling and the tower where she'd been kept cloaked in a golden glow. She could see The Shard, where they'd kept Jed, shining against the blackness of the sky. And between them both, lit by soft white light, she could see the Old Bailey Courts – the home of justice.

She turned and walked behind Jed, so that she could see the river, flooded with light spilling down from the cathedral.

Directly below them, the Millennium Bridge

extended across the water. Kassia could see the place where Jed had climbed out of the Thames nearly exactly a year ago.

From so high up and in the artificial light of the city at night, it looked like the river was still. A sheet of cut-glass stretching through London and down towards the sea. But she knew that currents churned below the surface.

'You can never step into the same river twice,' she said quietly.

Jed squeezed her hand in his. 'You're not supposed to,' he said.

It was cold and the wind bit at her face and she shivered. 'Where is the elixir, Jed?'

Jed led her towards the other side of the balcony. He stopped on the walkway. At their feet, a small, square hole had been cut in the metal and the hole had been covered with glass. 'Look down,' he said.

Her heart flipped inside her. Was it here? Was this where the elixir was hidden?

There was no pocket watch or glass bottle. All Kassia could see was what looked like an enormous star filling the space in the square. 'What is that?'

'The floor of the cathedral,' said Jed.

Kassia leant closer. It looked miles away, so small and contained and yet when they had been down in the main building the space had seemed huge.

'Notice the square surround?' he said.

Kassia had no idea why this was important. 'The final shape in the puzzle,' he said. 'On the Whispering Gallery, the triangles that allowed sound to carry. On the Stone Gallery, the circle that curved round without end. And then here. At the very top, on the Golden Gallery, a square. Together, they make the mark of the Brothers of Heliopolis.'

Kassia recognised the elements of the mark. But she didn't really understand why Jed was pointing them out to her.

'The elixir, Jed.' She was determined to bring him back on track. 'You said it was here.'

'It is. But first of all I want you to look down one more time at the star.'

'Why?'

Jed took a while before he answered. 'Because I want this place to be our place beside the river. Understand?'

It was what they had promised each other in Paris, that if ever they were separated, or if ever things went wrong, then they would find each other at the side of the river. That good things would happen.

Kassia stared down at the star and it was difficult to breathe.

Finally, Jed stood and she pulled herself up to face him. 'It's time now,' he said.

Relief flooded through every part of her. 'You're going to get the elixir?'

He nodded. 'I want you to wait just inside, OK?'

She wanted to argue. They'd come this far together and now at the very end he wanted to be alone. She looked out over the metal handrail and the twinkling view of the city. 'You're not going to do anything stupid?' she asked.

'Just wait for me,' he said.

Kassia stepped through the door into the main building of the cathedral. And she waited. She counted to ten in her head to try and stop the panic pushing against the bottom of her lungs. She squeezed her eyes closed hoping that in the darkness the time would move quickly. But it slowed. And so she opened her eyes. She saw Jed, standing in the doorway to the balcony, the glow from the cathedral illuminations fanning out from his shoulders, bathing him in light.

He held his hand up. And Kassia could see his fingers tightly gripped around something small.

Relief flooded through her. Jed had the elixir.

'Let's go back down to meet the others,' Jed said. He took Kassia's hand and they began to descend.

At the bottom of the stairs, Victor was waiting.

'Finally!' he blurted. 'Took your time up there, mate! It's nearly eleven o'clock!'

The edges of Jed's lips twitched into a nervous smile. 'There were things that needed to be done,' he said.

'You have the elixir?' Victor mumbled. 'Because you do not want to go upsetting these people.'

Jed held the bottle up so Victor could see. The elixir drifted in circles. A golden cloud against the glass.

Victor nodded and reached for Jed's extended arm and repositioned the restraint cuff around his wrist. 'Let's do this, then,' he said.

And as Jed pulled his arm away, he said thank you.

The three of them walked towards where Montgomery and the others were waiting. Their footsteps rang out loudly on the flagstones. But Kassia was aware of another noise. A frantic thumping at the West Door.

'See to that!' yelled Montgomery, his patience clearly worn thin by Jed and Kassia's journey to the top of the cathedral.

Reverend Cockren hurried to the door and pulled it open a crack. But those on the other side forced against it and tumbled inside. Dante and Giseppi and Amelie.

'Well, well, well!' moaned Montgomery. 'You just couldn't keep away, could you?'

Dante signed wildly in Kassia's direction.

'I'm OK. I'm OK. They didn't hurt me.' This wasn't entirely true but it didn't really seem like a good idea to tell Dante about the surges of electricity. He looked more than a little rattled.

Her brother exhaled loudly as if it was the first time he had been able to breathe properly since being left behind in Herne Bay.

'And you, Fulcanelli?' said Giseppi. 'They did not do the hurting of you?'

Jed shook his head. 'I'm fine.'

Dante wobbled where he stood, fighting back exhaustion. 'We've been searching all of London,' his fingers blurted. 'Mum, Nat and Charlie are trying Postman's Park again. Where have you been?'

Kassia couldn't begin to explain about the Star Chamber and the clock tower. But she knew, anyway, her brother's question was really about whether Jed had found the elixir. About whether he'd been able to take it.

What could she answer when she had no idea what was happening herself? Her fingers wouldn't work to find the words she needed. Suddenly she felt an overwhelming sadness that her mum wasn't here and that she was still out in the city searching for them.

'So where exactly are we up to?' pressed on Giseppi. 'Because there have been sections of this drama that my friends and I did not do the seeing of.'

'Fulcanelli is about to hand over the elixir,' said Montgomery greedily. 'After all this time and after all our chasing, he is finally going to give us our prize.'

Jed held up the bottle so that everyone could see it. A hush fell over the cathedral. It would have been possible to hear a clock ticking.

'You need to release Kassia from the restraints first,' Jed said, shattering the silence.

Montgomery laughed. 'You think I'm stupid? All the time you and she wear the restraints, Victor can hurt you. When I have the elixir in my hand, only *then* will I release your friend.'

Victor looked across at Kassia.

'You need to let Jed go too,' Kassia said. Her mind was whirring. Would that work? If Jed handed over the elixir then how would he take it himself? This was getting too muddled. Time was too tight. 'But first he needs to take a final dose,' she blurted.

Jed stepped closer to stop her saying any more. 'Do everything I say,' he whispered again.

She had promised to do that. But this plan was making no sense. Jed had to take the elixir. There was less than an hour until the year was up. He couldn't hand it over now. Whatever his plan was, it couldn't possibly work in the time.

'Please!' she yelled, hurrying towards Montgomery. 'Let him take the elixir. We will find a way of making more!'

Montgomery cut the air with his cane and Kassia stumbled backwards. 'Fulcanelli does not need the elixir. He is invincible. We have seen that. You have seen that!'

'No. It's more complicated!' Kassia wailed.

'Kassia, please!' Jed called from behind her. 'You have to trust me!'

But what he was doing didn't fit together.

Jed held the bottle high and the elixir swirled. 'Now we will do things my way,' he said calmly.

Carter lurched forward to grab him. Jed pulled away, the bottle still raised in his hand.

'Come near again and I will drop it,' Jed yelled.

Montgomery tugged Carter backwards and lurched towards Victor. 'The restraint!' he yelled. 'Press the button.'

Victor lifted his arms, slid back the cuff of his sleeve, and his wrist was bare. The metal cuff he'd worn earlier, missing now. 'The system is deactivated,' he said calmly. 'The chain is broken.'

Kassia had no time to process this. When had Victor removed the cuff? Why had he done that? Why didn't he want to hurt them any more?

She could see from the way Montgomery's face distorted and creased that the same questions were pummelling inside his brain. All the certainty he'd had drained away. He staggered forward, leaning his weight on his stick, his teeth gritted against the anger that obviously raged inside him. Carter made a grab for Victor, but Jed raised the bottle higher over the flagstone floor.

'OK, OK,' Montgomery stuttered eventually. 'Your terms, Fulcanelli.'

What was Jed doing? There was only half an hour left. Was he really going to hand the elixir over? 'Jed, please!' Kassia sobbed.

'We need to go outside,' said Jed forcefully.

'Hold on a minute,' snapped Carter. 'If we go outside, you'll run.'

So that was the plan. Kassia could see how this would work. Jed would make a run for it.

Jed stood his ground. 'We do this outside beside the river where I first clambered out of the water. Or I drop the bottle here and your precious elixir does nothing more than stain the stones we stand on.'

Montgomery looked across at Martha Quinn.

Jed lifted his hand even higher.

'Fine,' blurted Montgomery. 'Outside, beside the river.'

Reverend Cockren opened the West Door of the cathedral and then the nine of them proceeded behind him down the steps, past the grassy area where the statue of John Donne stood, across the walkway that led to the Millennium Bridge, and eventually to the edge of the water and the steps that led into the Thames.

Kassia tried to push forward. 'Take it now, Jed!' she shouted, tears stinging in her eyes, panic ripping at her chest. 'Jed! Please!'

Jed stood with his back to the river. He lifted the bottle.

Kassia knew that after all this time and all this agony, the time for making his immortality permanent had arrived.

Jed lifted the other hand. Kassia knew he was going to reach for the cork. He was going to break the seal of the bottle. He was going to drink.

Jed looked through the gaggle of people, past Dante and Amelie and Giseppi and the people who had hunted him across time. And he focused only on her.

Jed gripped his empty hand into a fist. Then he moved his fist in the shape of a circle across his chest, wincing as the pressure caught against his scars.

With a sickening blow to the stomach, Kassia read the sign that he was making.

It was the sign for 'sorry'.

Why was he sorry? What was he doing? 'Jed, please!' she screamed, the words ripping at the back of her throat. 'I want you to live for ever!'

His eyes stayed locked on hers and he reached out with the hand that had made the sign. He snapped the wax that covered the cork in the neck of the bottle.

He *was* going to drink! Everything would be OK! Breath funnelled into her lungs. She strained forward.

Kassia wasn't the only one who moved towards the edge of the river.

'Stop him!' yelled Montgomery, raising his cane and slicing through the air as if it was a sword.

Carter and Montgomery flung themselves at Jed.

Jed arched his back. He fixed his gaze, his eyes never moving from Kassia's. He tipped his hand. The bottle angled over the water.

'No!' Montgomery bellowed. The walking cane severed the air again. This time it connected with Jed's side.

For a second, Jed doubled over, one hand flickering and clutching at nothing, the other extended above the water, the bottle leaning back, the elixir swirling like gathering, golden cloud.

There was a moment of recoil as Jed lurched up, both hands now flung wide, head tipped back. He closed his eyes.

Kassia reached to grab him.

She was too late.

Jed's body fell, arms spread wide, one gripped tightly to the bottle of elixir.

And the water of the River Thames surged up to claim them both.

Kassia screamed like she had never screamed before. She broke her way through the group, crashing against Montgomery.

This could not be happening. It was a mistake. Jed had opened the bottle. He must have drunk the elixir. He must have planned his escape! He had said to trust him. To do exactly as he said – and now he had fallen into the water.

She charged along the walkway that ran beside the river. She could see Jed's body, floating, arms still stretched wide as the water pummelled around him. He had to have had a plan! There had to be a reason!

She was aware of someone running just behind her. She didn't turn to see who it was. She just focused on the river. On Jed's body being carried by the tide.

Every step was agony. Her heart was hurting in her chest and she couldn't pull in enough air to fill her lungs. She did not slow her pace. And whoever it was behind her, kept pace with her every stride.

There was a break in the river wall. A flight of stairs that led down to a beach beside the water. She scrambled and stumbled, her arms pumping as she ran.

Her feet sank into the sand. She kicked through debris and driftwood, the ground like mud, trying to pull her downwards.

She hurled herself towards the edge of the water. It was icy cold and it took what breath she had and froze it in the back of her throat.

If she wasn't quicker, the tide would carry Jed from her, away towards the sea.

She sprinted into the depths of the river, churning the water through her hands and screaming out. She begged the Thames to hear her and hold his body till she could reach him.

And someone swam beside her. Dante. His feet kicked with hers and his hands pummelled through the water too.

The waves reached up for her. They tugged her under. She scratched her hands towards the surface. The water flickered and pulsed. And Kassia screamed out into the wind.

Some people believe that when you drown, your whole life flashes before you. The boy in the river saw only bottles, driftwood and the dented licence plate of a foreign car. Not his life. But he knew for certain that he was drowning.

He wanted to swallow, but the muscles in his throat constricted. His whole neck and jaw, vice tight. He was pretty sure that his lungs were ripping open. A searing pain pierced his nostrils and his eyes were grazed with grit. He was heavier now and the surface was retreating every second, so that the light that rippled in circles over his head was getting further away.

His time was up.

And then, through the water, he saw a face, hair flailed out behind her. A girl reached for him. Light pulsed from his fingers. As she grabbed his hand, it was as if the water that pressed him down exploded with colour and light.

Memories coursed up from somewhere deep inside him. *Ice skates gliding across a rink; pastries outside a Parisian café; a seat on a balcony looking up at a sea of stars; a sponge cake decorated with frosting; a mug of steaming hot chocolate; a silver pocket watch with a swallow engraved on the casing; a sugar bird with a broken wing.*

The boy saw his life.

He punched his hand through the surface. He

forced his chin up into the light and gulped. River waterfalled into his throat. He was sure his chest would explode. A wave dragged him under again and flung him hard against the bank. Hands closed over his. And the river fell away behind him, clinging to its cargo of bottles, paper and cans, carrying them down towards the sea.

He was on dry land. The fight was over and the boy had won.

He lay with his face pressed against the beach. He could still hear the river. And he could hear the sounds of a city moving all around him.

Hands turned him over, heaving him on to his back. He looked up.

Kassia looked down at him.

And he knew now exactly who and where he was.

Dante scooped Jed up and carried him across the beach to a breakwater that jutted from the sand. He knelt down and lowered Jed's body so that his back was resting against the wooden posts, slumped as if Jed had chosen to relax here for a moment by the riverside and admire the view.

Then Dante stepped away, steering Kassia towards Jed. 'I'll be just here,' he signed.

Kassia stumbled to her knees and flung herself

forward so that her body pressed against Jed's. She tried to mumble his name over and over. But no sound came. All she could hear was his heartbeat. All she could feel was his chest, rising and falling in ragged breaths.

She clutched for his hand. It flickered and faded, his whole body washed in light and distortion making him look something like a hologram. A projection somehow, diluted by the river.

In his hand there was a bottle. Kassia unlocked the fingers and peeled them away from the glass. The bottle was empty of golden cloud. It swirled instead with dirty water from the Thames.

'Tell me you drank it,' she screamed at him. 'Tell me, Jed! That you took the elixir before it was too late!'

She rocked back on her heels to hear his answer. She could see now that his shirt was ripped and tattered. The branding of the dragon flickered, as if lit from inside his body.

Jed shook his head. He gripped his empty hand into a fist and he rubbed it again, in the shape of a circle, across the scars.

'No!' Kassia screamed, thumping her hand down into the sand. 'Don't tell me you're sorry! Tell me you took the elixir!'

'I didn't, Kass.'

'So we'll find more,' she cried. 'We'll go to the hospital. Nat will help us. Find some way to make you stable until we can work this out and make things right.'

'I didn't take it, because I chose not to,' he said calmly.

She let the bottle tumble free. Dirty water rushed out, scoring a rivulet into the sand.

'But why?' she pleaded. 'You had eternal life there in your hands!'

He clutched at his chest and the brand there flickered and pulsed. 'We are all eternal already,' he mumbled.

His face seemed to glow. A light lifted up from his hands and his chest and it flickered and faltered, but his eyes burned brightly and they fixed on her.

'I don't understand!' she sobbed, tears scorching her skin.

'We are all made of water,' Jed said. 'I returned the elixir to the river. It was the real start of the adventure, not St Paul's, after all. I put it back where it belonged.'

'You're wrong!' she stammered. 'The elixir was yours. It was meant for you!'

He struggled to pull himself up against the breakwater. The light throbbed and stuttered. 'Maybe chasing the elixir was something which was meant for me. But I wasn't meant to take it. I know that now.'

'But all our hunting? All our searching?'

'Was about looking. It wasn't about what we found.'

Kassia drove her hands against his chest. His scars buckled and crumpled in the light. 'No!' she screamed.

He grabbed her arm. He held it tight. And he made her look at him.

The light lifted and pulsed, swirling and stretching as if he was behind a pane of mottled glass.

'It was about chasing time, Kass. But we got everything backwards.'

'How?' she cried.

'We had a year, and all I did was try and extend that time when I should have been focusing on the days that I had. The days that *we* had.'

'What did we have?'

'We had friends. We had family. We had the people who tried to help us. People of all ages and from all kinds of places, all there for us. And I . . .' He folded into a wave of pain that pushed out from his chest and rippled through his body. 'I had you.'

'And all I wanted to do was to help you!'

'You *did* help me!' He pulled himself up and put his hand on her cheek. The fingers flickered and faded. The light from Jed's chest tugged at them both like water dragging them under. All she could see was him. 'You helped me more than you will ever know.'

His hand felt wet against her skin and she couldn't tell if it was tears from her eyes, blood from the lifeline on his palm, or water from the river.

He pressed his forehead against hers. His breath rattled in his chest as he spoke to her. 'Please don't hate me, Kassia. I just found different answers than the one we thought I needed.'

The pressure of his forehead against hers felt heavier suddenly, as if he was leaning into her and drawing strength from her in order to breathe.

'I could never hate you, Jed,' she spluttered, and the words caught in her throat as she tried to speak again. 'I love you.'

There was a backdraught of light. Kassia was thrown sideways as wind spiralled in from the river. The light gushed upwards like a geyser in the desert. It formed a funnel that circled and pulsated, spinning faster and faster, drilling into the air. The circle thickened and widened, growing and changing as the body of a golden dragon formed in front of her. It spun round and round, and the mouth of the dragon reached for its tail. But the mouth stayed open and the tail flicked free so that the dragon stretched out to form a shape like an arrow. It extended upwards from the riverbank and it filled the air with light and colour. Then it buckled like it was being drawn backwards on the string of a bow, firing up and straining for the moon, before exploding into a torrent of stars across a darkening sky.

Kassia fell back on to the sand. Grit pressed against her face. Water from the river lapped at her feet.

And when she opened her eyes and sat up, she and Dante were alone on the beach.

Jed was gone.

DAY 366

28th February

Kassia was suddenly aware of arms around her. Dante cradled her against him.

She fought to get free, scratching at his arms and kicking against the ground as he dragged her up to stand with him. Still he held on.

Jed had gone. She had to find him. Needed to reach him.

But Dante's arms were locked around her, as tight as the restraint she wore around her wrist.

Though she knew Dante couldn't hear her, she yelled at him to release her, digging her nails into his arms and kicking her feet against the sand.

But he did not let go.

Until the storm that raged under her skin had lessened and they fell again to their knees on the beach and Kassia pressed her hand into the shingle.

315

The Topkapı Dagger
The handle and the case of the dagger are made of gold. The handle is ornamented with emerald stones and topped by a watch. The emerald lid of the watch opens when the knob is pressed. The dagger was sent by Sultan Mahmud I (1730-1754) to the Persian ruler Nader Shah as a gift. Upon Nader Shah's death, the Ottoman mission brought the dagger and other gifts back to the palace.

Minutes passed. Hours, maybe. It felt like days.

Kassia twisted round to face her brother.

And she saw that they were not alone any more. Giseppi and Amelie and Reverend Cockren stood in a line behind her. Hurrying towards them were Montgomery, Carter, Martha Quinn and Victor.

Montgomery burst between Giseppi and Amelie and fell to his knees, reaching for the fallen bottle. 'Where is it?' he bellowed. 'Where is he?'

It was Reverend Cockren who answered. 'Both are gone,' he said.

As Montgomery twisted the empty bottle in his hand, Kassia scrambled upright. 'He was here!' she yelled. 'He was here and now—'

Reverend Cockren stepped towards her. 'His time was up, Kassia.'

Anger flared inside her. She launched herself at Giseppi. 'You!' she screamed. 'You are a Brother of Heliopolis! You were supposed to keep the elixir safe. You were supposed to help him!'

Giseppi grabbed her hands. 'We did! We did!' he said frantically.

'Then why is he gone?' she screamed, tugging her arms free and plunging her hands into her soaking wet hair.

'He did the readings of all the signs,' said Giseppi.

'He saw all the messages and, finally, in the end, he did the realising that living for ever wasn't something that he could do.'

'But all of our searching,' she pleaded. 'It was for the elixir.'

'It was for answers,' said Giseppi. 'And his final answer wasn't the one for which you did the hoping.'

Kassia stumbled. The world felt like it was spinning. Behind her, Montgomery rocked backwards and forwards on his knees, calling out in words that she couldn't properly hear because her mind couldn't focus.

Kassia turned. 'You!' she screamed at Victor. 'You and everyone at NOAH,' she said, waving her hands at Martha Quinn, Montgomery and Carter who were all kneeling now, the empty bottle passing between them. 'If you hadn't demanded the elixir, he would have taken it. He would still be here.'

Victor shook his head. 'Is that really what happened?' he said, as she floundered in front of him. 'It looked to me as if Jed made a choice.'

Kassia couldn't make sense of what Victor was saying, though the words he spoke were clear.

'He made sure you were free before he made his decision.'

'I don't understand!' she bellowed.

Reverend Cockren moved between them. He was holding a book in his hands and he offered it to her.

'What's that?' she yelled, batting it away.

'John Donne's poetry,' the Reverend said quietly.

Kassia could not contain the anger that roiled inside her. 'Him!' she screamed. 'The guy whose statue guarded the elixir? What good is that to me?'

'Jed found answers there,' said the Reverend.

'Jed found the elixir!' Kassia yelled.

'Please,' Reverend Cockren said quietly, the book wavering a little in his hand. 'It might help you understand.'

'Your father offered books like this to Jed, years ago,' added Victor.

Now Kassia thought her heart would stop beating. 'My dad! What has this – today – what Jed did – have to do with my dad? I don't understand what you're saying!'

'You will, in time,' said Reverend Cockren.

She spun round to face him. 'Don't talk to me about time! We had a year! And he *had* the elixir! He could have taken it before! And now it's too late!' She folded forward, the words that had been holding her up, released now, so that all her power had gone.

'That's the point,' said Reverend Cockren. 'Jed could have taken the elixir when he first found it. But in the end, he chose not to. None of this will make sense until you can look up clearly at all that happened.'

The words muddled in Kassia's head. But one phrase jolted in her brain. 'Look up.'

And suddenly she understood. Jed wasn't dead at all. He'd promised her he'd live for ever. When they'd been climbing up to the galleries inside the cathedral. He had said he would be with her when she skated and drank hot chocolate on the street. This was all part of the plan. A trick to make NOAH leave them alone. She was furious with herself for doubting and not trusting.

She looked across at Montgomery, Carter and Martha Quinn, who still scrabbled on the sand, trying to salvage something of their hopes and dreams for answers. But Kassia knew somehow that the answer would not be here beside the river. To find the answer she would need to look up. To find Jed, she needed to be at St Paul's.

She pushed past her brother and the others, and scrambled up the steps away from the beach. If they followed, she couldn't hear them. If they were behind her, they couldn't catch her. Because she ran faster than she'd ever run before.

Her arms pumped the air. Her legs cramped. Her feet thudded on the pavement.

It was dark but she could see clearly now. Jed would be waiting for her. He would be in the cathedral. He wasn't gone at all. He was just waiting.

She raced past the break in the wall where he had risen from the Thames; she pushed her way up the path to the cathedral and she charged up the steps towards the West Door. She grabbed the handle and tugged the door open and burst into the nave, her feet echoing on the flagstones.

Her side ached. Her head pounded. Her breath was catching and spluttering in the space between her lungs and mouth, burning at her throat. None of that mattered. Because she knew where she was going. And she knew Jed would be waiting.

She hurried past a statue of a man wrapped in death cloths and thundered towards the entrance to the stairs. She began to climb.

As she got higher, she counted the steps. It kept her focused. Kept her on course. He would be in the Whispering Gallery, she knew it. The place where, even far away from her, she could hear his every word.

She barrelled through the door that opened to the gallery. The balcony ringing the space above the Cornhill paintings, where he had talked about Elymas and his magic. But this was different. Jed was different. Jed would be here.

322

The Whispering Gallery was empty. There was no one there.

Kassia flopped down on the stone seats. She leant her head against the wall. It was OK. It was going to be OK. She angled her ear to the cold stone of the wall and tried to breathe. And it was as if she heard Jed talking, words carrying through the wall and soaking into her.

And she knew, with even more certainty than before, that he would be waiting. Not in this gallery then, but on the next. The one of stone.

She pulled herself up and she drove on towards the stairs.

She took the steps two at a time, grasping the handrail, her legs trembling, muscles twitching in her calves. But she did not slow down.

He would be on the Stone Gallery.

She thrust open the door that led to the outside of the cathedral. 'Jed!' she yelled, running around the walkway. 'Jed!'

He had to be here. All the stone stories they had read. All the images and stone symbols they had pieced together. He had to be here.

But she circled the gallery alone. There was no one else.

She doubled over and pressed her forehead against

her knees and tried not to be sick.

Then she shook herself because she could not believe she could be so stupid. Why would he wait for her on either of these balconies? When they had been here only hours before, he had explained that it was the third level that was most important. He had to be on the Golden Gallery. That is where he would wait for her.

Pulling all the strength she could from deep inside her, she charged towards the final staircase. The stairs were narrower. The ceiling pressed in like a tunnel leading from a cave. Her legs were so wobbly she had to focus to put one foot in front of the other. But none of that mattered, because she was getting closer. She was nearly at the top of the cathedral. Their place beside the river, Jed had said. She knew now this was where he'd be.

She pushed open the door.

The air was cold on her face. The night sky, dark, lit by stars and a glowing full moon.

Kassia pressed her hand against the wall of the cathedral. She ran towards the metal railing that kept her from tumbling into the city far below.

She could hardly breathe. She wasn't sure she had the strength to speak. But she opened her mouth and sound ripped upwards, broken and stuttering as she called Jed's name over and over.

She circled the gallery. She retraced her steps to the door.

With a cold and tightening sense of reality, Kassia realised Jed wasn't here.

She sank to the ground. Her hands pressed either side of the square of glass that had been cut into the path. She gazed down at the star pattern on the floor of the cathedral. And she began to cry.

Jed wasn't here.

She had been so sure. So positive it was all a mistake. He had promised he wouldn't leave her. But he had. She realised, with a jolt that rocked inside her, that Jed was really gone.

She wasn't sure how long she stayed there, looking down into the cathedral. But it was until her back ached and her arms were rigid with cold and exhaustion. Finally, she eased herself on to her heels and looked up.

And it was then she saw it.

Attached to the metal railing round the gallery, moving gently in the breeze, was a single red rose.

She rubbed her face with the back of her hand and narrowed her eyes, trying to see more clearly. Jed? Had he left it for her? When he had asked her to wait inside the stairwell while he'd collected the elixir hours before? Was the rose from him? Was it meant for her?

Kassia got up and walked slowly towards the rose and untied it. It was only then that she saw there was something else attached to the stem. A silver pocket watch glinting in the light of the stars.

Kassia twisted the wire that held the rose and watch in place, and then sank back to her knees. She detached the watch from the stem of the rose and she twisted it over and over in her hand. Her father's pocket watch, engraved with the mark of the swallow. A single bird in flight.

This watch had been everywhere with them. It had registered every minute and counted down every hour. And Jed had used it to store the elixir. Time frozen to make space for eternity.

With shaking fingers, Kassia slid her thumbnail into the tiny catch that held the watch case closed. The back section sprung open.

Inside the void, where time and forever had both been stored, there was a folded piece of paper.

She lifted it out of the casing.

The paper was as thin as tissue, creased again and again, and as she unfolded it Kassia could see that the paper was covered in tiny writing. The words had been pressed and scrunched together, covering every available section of space.

Under the glow of the moon and the coloured light that flooded the cathedral, she began to read.

Dear Kass,

OK, so well done for knowing where to come. And sorry if for a moment you thought that I would be waiting here in person for you. We've seen so many weird and crazy things together that perhaps that is what you hoped. So I'm sorry.

But I am here really. All around you. In the rose I left, although maybe you'll think that's kind of soppy. And in the river that runs around the cathedral. And in the stars that I hope you'll see above you. It will be kind of sad if you don't make it here until daylight. But in a way that won't matter either. Because the stars are always there. Whether you can see them or not. So that's kind of beautiful.

I'm not sure I'm saying this right. Or explaining things in the way I should. You were better with words than me. And that part is important.

Do you remember the day I found your books and stories hidden in the bottom of your wardrobe? Wow, you were mad at me. Your face went all blotchy and you went kind of huffy and for a while I couldn't work out why it was you were so angry. But I think I've worked it out. I think it was because I'd found the way you and your dad had used words so powerfully and I think you were embarrassed because maybe I didn't get it.

But I've thought about those books and stories quite a lot over the last months or so. And today Reverend Cockren gave me a book of poetry. We were looking for the way to live for ever and he gave me a book of words. It made me think of the poetry book we found in the box. Apparently, a book of poems is what your dad tried to give me on the day of the fifth elixir. On the day he died.

I'm so sorry I didn't listen then, Kass. I'm sorry I wasn't sure what the poems meant when we found them. I'm so sorry that all this happened. In my fight to live for ever, lots of people got hurt and I know you said the disasters were not connected. But I've got to the point now where I can't be sure.

One of those poems by that John Donne guy said that no man is an island. That what we do affects other people. And those words had power. So I hope you understand why in the end I couldn't take the elixir. If I'd done that, NOAH would never have stopped chasing me. They are kind of crazed about finding solutions, aren't they? And we saw what happened to Jacob when he felt the elixir was his right to have. In the end I couldn't get my head round it. Who would set limits? Who would have made decisions about who lived and died? I think it would have got really messy. I don't think the world is ready for that yet. And I didn't want to be the one who gave them the chance to test it. I understood, in the end, that I wasn't an island. Sounds kind of weird, I know. But I think you'll understand that even better than I did.

And then there was something else I began to understand. The whole thing about change. When it came to it, I couldn't face the idea of never changing. Being fixed where I was. I suppose what I'm getting at is that I was scared of being fixed without you. I know. That's soppy too. But what would we have done? Would we have found a way for you to take elixir? Who else would we have given the chance to? And would we have been happy trapped, unmoving for ever, in time?

You see, as an alchemist, I knew that change was the thing that was important. And for a while I had forgotten it. But I remember the power of that now.

And knowing you *changed* me. The way you believed in me, the way you trusted, the way you risked so much. Bergier said a funny thing to us, didn't he, when we were in Paris? It didn't make sense then. But it does now. He talked about the philosopher's stone and he said, 'It's you, Fulcanelli.' I thought that was just because he'd recognised me. But it wasn't that at all. It was something more powerful than that. He knew the change had to happen inside me. And it did. Being with you and working together helped me make the change. I don't know if my heart changed from lead to gold exactly. But I know that the drive and the greed that pushed me on to chase the elixir, became something different. I think I changed in a good way.

But there was another reason. And it goes back to those poems and stories that you had hidden in a box and tried to forget.

I think we are eternal already, Kass. I think we can live for ever, even if we can't be seen, like those stars that hide but are always there. We spent our time looking for a phoenix man and I think, in the end, that was me. I know. Sounds kind of big headed. But I'm trying to make sense of that. I had so many chances to start again. I think it was best just to let the fire change me in a different way. And I think the power of our story will live on in the words about it. That would be good. It's what I hope.

In reality, I have no idea what will happen after I give up the chance to take the elixir. I have no idea what is after all this. Maybe nothing. Maybe something more. But I think it might be an adventure, and so I think this is the right thing to do. It's important you know it's not that I've given up. It's more that I realise that what is right for me, for you, for everyone, is that the year ends. And I don't take the final dose. I think there's a power in that and I hope you can see it.

I hope you'll forgive me.

I guess for a while you might be really mad. Maybe all blotchy faced and huffy again, like you were about me finding your stories. I'm sorry I couldn't explain it when we were together. I couldn't really find the words I needed then and we might have argued and you would have interrupted and got all cross. But writing the words is easier somehow. The writing makes sense of what I'm thinking and although I'm nervous, I want you to know, that I'm sure. And I was sure of nothing when I clambered out of the Thames. But a year with you and it's finally made sense to me.

There was one final piece of the puzzle. Another story that

we heard together. Do you remember the Topkapi dagger? It was pretty special, wasn't it, with its emeralds and its hidden clock? But the part of the story that was important was that the dagger was given away, and that it was never used and so it was returned. We found the elixir, Kass. But that didn't mean that taking it was right. Which is why I made a decision to hand it back.

So, if things went as I planned them to, the elixir has gone into the river, washed away to the sea. That makes sense to me. Because the water will move in a cycle, round and round like that spinning dragon we saw so often. Because life is like that, isn't it? A circle. And the power of our story is that we are all connected.

I'm sorry. I've waffled on. If the stars were visible when you started reading this, then they've probably disappeared now. But they are still there, Kass. And I am still here. I promised I would never leave you. And I meant that. Just not, I guess, in the way that you hoped.

I expect it will be difficult for a while. I never wanted that. But if you skate and make cakes and remember me sometimes (without getting too sad!) then I think that will help.

I think it will help, too, if you write stories. I kind of think that is what you were always supposed to do. I know there was a time that you thought you could only help people and mend them if you were a doctor. And that's great and everything. But I think you are supposed to use words to heal people. That might sound a bit preachy but if this is my last chance to tell you what I think, then I think you should give it a go.

And so I have again run out of time. The story of our lives, don't you reckon? Racing time. Maybe the lesson of our story is that we should try and focus on the individual minutes as we live them and not the final destination at all. I hope you get to do that, Kassia, because I think you're going to be in for quite an adventure if you do.

Thank you for helping me. Thank you for trusting me.

Just thank you, really.

You might not want me to say this now. But I think the colour of the rose says it anyway.

I love you.

Jed

GOLDEN GALLERY
85m from Cathedral Floor
528 steps up

STONE GALLERY
53m from Cathedral Floor
376 steps up

WHISPERING GALLERY
30m from Cathedral Floor
7 steps up

CATHEDRAL FLOOR

CRYPT

D FULCANELLI

FRIEND OF MANY

WHO GAVE UP THE CHANCE
LIVE FOREVER TO SHOW US
NOT TO BE AFRAID, BUT
INSTEAD TO LIVE FULLY.

BRUARY · 28TH · 20

DAY 1
29th February

Kassia had no idea how many hours she stayed on the walkway of the Golden Gallery. Morning came. The city woke. It lived its day. And Kassia read the letter over and over until she knew it off by heart. Then she folded the piece of paper and tucked it tightly back inside the casing of her father's pocket watch.

And sleep overwhelmed her.

When she finally woke, the day they had been counting down to for so long had passed entirely. Her fingers were still gripped tightly round the watch, her fingertips resting on the engraving of the swallow. A bird in flight, coming home.

Kassia stood and tucked the watch inside her pocket. She walked over to the metal railings that ran round the gallery.

It was no longer dark. It was not yet light. A smear

of sunrise was emerging over the river. The stars still sparkling, but harder to see. A bridge between one day and another. And she stood on the bridge and she looked down at the Thames.

She realised as she watched that today was a leap day. An extra day added to the end of the year. An extra pocket of time. And she smiled.

EPILOGUE
1st March – One year later

It was early morning. Postman's Park was nearly deserted. Even the sun was barely awake.

A small group of people stood huddled together under the overhanging canopy in the far corner of the park.

Kassia held a long-stemmed flower in her hand.

'I like your bracelet,' signed Dante.

Kassia laughed. 'Better than the one I was wearing this time a year ago,' she signed back.

This bracelet was made of silver. A simple solid band that snaked around her wrist and appeared to have no beginning and no end. A single silver charm hung from it. A tiny silver swallow in flight. One wing was slightly crooked. A second bird like the one engraved on the back of her father's pocket watch. It was a reminder of a sugar bird made so long ago. And it was a symbol she'd heard about from her father. A swallow like the one a sailor would have inked into a tattoo when they set off on a voyage, to be joined by another when he returned home. In certain lights, when the sun caught on the silver, the swallow looked like a phoenix. A bird reborn from the flames.

Dante stamped his feet against the cold and folded his arm across himself.

Beside him, on the other side, Amelie leant forward. She used her hands to speak, adding spoken words only out of habit. 'How is your writing going?' she asked.

Kassia nodded and signed back. 'OK, I think. I'm trying to write our story.'

Amelie laughed. 'Don't forget the part in the scwers!'

'I won't forget any of it,' said Kassia.

Anna and Nat stepped a little closer so their signs could be seen by all who sheltered underneath the canopy. 'She's going to use words to help people fix themselves,' Anna said proudly.

'Well, I think she will do better at that than being a doctor,' laughed Nat. 'But if she changes her mind, she can have my job at the hospital.'

'Hey! Don't you go abandoning me to the mercies

of that mad consultant in charge of A&E!' groaned Charlie. 'I need you there to dilute his anger.'

'Oh, I'm glad my disasters help you out!' said Nat.

Kassia watched the two of them. She felt a stab of something that might have been regret. Or maybe it was a twinge of fear. She wasn't sure she could do this writing thing as well as everyone hoped. She guessed that knowing you were doing the right thing didn't mean that you'd automatically be free of worries about it.

Suddenly, she was aware of footsteps behind her.

Victor and Giseppi had come through the gates of the park.

'Sorry!' winced Giseppi. 'Victor here was doing the celebrating of his birthday last night.'

Victor looked rather sheepish and rubbed his hand across his hair. 'Yep. Soz about that.'

'It's OK,' said Kassia. 'I think Jed would have liked that. In fact, I *know* he would.'

Victor nodded gratefully and lowered his hand. 'Last birthday kind of passed me by.'

'I bet it did, after a stand-off with NOAH,' said Kassia, angling her head to the side. 'Have you still heard nothing from them since Martha Quinn dumped your clothes from the top balcony of The Shard?'

Victor grinned at the memory. 'Pretty unarguable way to make it clear my services were no longer needed, don't you think?'

'You don't have any regrets?' pressed Kassia.

'What, giving up the chance to live in a penthouse room in a city in the sky so I can live in a leaky narrowboat moored on Regent's Canal instead? What is there to regret?'

'Hey, mate!' cut in Charlie. 'Fixing damage doubles as your rent. The leaks are yours.'

'He's good at fixing damage,' Kassia said defensively.

Victor pulled a small box of toffees out of his pocket. It was a little bashed on one side, but Kassia beamed as she took it.

'There's seriously been no follow-up from Montgomery or Carter?' asked Nat.

'NOAH is a huge organisation,' said Victor. 'Department Nine was all about Fulcanelli. But there were other departments, all searching for ways to achieve Absolute Health. So of course they weren't happy. But I think they'll just be channelling their efforts into other ways to live for ever. They'll be chasing other people and other ideas now. I think we're off the hook.' He grinned. 'But I kind of think *they* might not be. All the power of the government can't keep what they did quiet. From what I hear, the police are closing in. They will pay for it.'

Kassia nodded gratefully. There was a chance, then, that their dads would finally get justice.

'So show them the tattoo,' urged Charlie.

Victor rolled up his sleeve. The unicorn was still there, but the chain around its leg was faded, almost disappeared.

'You're just getting rid of the chain, then?' asked Amelie.

Victor shivered against the cold and pulled the sleeve down. 'Sure. I don't want to forget the unicorn, but like Reverend Cockren said, there was a reason the unicorn missed the ark.'

There was a moment of silence, unbroken by sound or signs. Kassia knew the reason. It was choice. And even though she still felt massive pain, and even though she sometimes woke up in the night to find herself crying, she accepted it. She had begun to understand it.

'Talking of the Reverend,' said Giseppi. 'Where is he? Wasn't he the one who said we had to be here by seven?'

'I am here,' came a voice from behind them. 'Just because you couldn't see me, didn't mean I wasn't.'

Kassia gripped a little more tightly to the stem of the flower in her hand.

'So,' said Reverend Cockren, stepping through the group so that he had his back to the wall that ran under the canopy. 'Are we ready?'

Kassia nodded and the group moved closer together so that the tiles on the wall behind the Reverend could be clearly read. Kassia knew most of the names there off by heart. Alice Ayers; Herbert Peter Cazaly; Thomas Griffin; Sarah Smith. She knew what they'd done and the sacrifices they'd made. But they were just names. She couldn't really feel the pain that their families and friends must have felt at their loss. Or the agony of their questions and their anger at the unfairness. Or their sense of pride that those they lost were prepared to do the right thing. But she had an idea now.

Reverend Cockren allowed a moment of quiet before he began to read a poem. This, too, Kassia knew by heart. She spoke every word along with him, inside her head.

Reverend Cockren reached behind him, to a space at the end of the line of plaques and memorials. A piece of blue velvet had been tacked to the wall. It covered a single tile. A new memorial amongst those for everyday heroes.

Reverend Cockren detached the cover and Kassia saw for the first time the tile in its final resting place. It was long and white and along each side was a decoration. On one there was symbol of a square and a triangle and a circle. And on the other there was a dragon. At first glance it looked as if the dragon was an ouroboros, but if you looked carefully you could see that the dragon's mouth didn't quite lock around its tail.

Between the two images, there was writing.

JED FULCANELLI
Friend of many

Who gave up the chance to live forever to show us not to be afraid, but instead to live fully.

February 28th 2016

'Live fully,' said Anna quietly, reaching for her daughter's hand. 'I like that.'

Kassia squeezed her mum's fingers. So did she.

Kassia stepped forward. She took the flower she'd been holding and knelt down and put it on the ground in front of the plaque. A single red rose. A symbol of alchemical completion. And a symbol of love.

As the sun rose further into the sky casting the first rays of spring, and the chance to awaken new life, Kassia and her friends and family turned and made their way towards the gates of the park.

'Where are you going now?' asked Victor.

'Fleet Street,' said Kassia. 'The street of ink. Then perhaps for a walk by the river. I'll probably stop for hot chocolate,' she added.

Victor smiled and Kassia said her goodbyes.

And she made her way into the city, ready now to face the adventures of a brand new day.

Read on to find out more about the real-life events which inspired this series!

Author's Note

River of Ink is a work of fiction . . . but it was inspired by some fascinating real events, real places and real people. So much of the fun of putting the series together came from mixing together truths from the real world with things I made up . . . and it might surprise you to know how much of the story was *not* invented.

For a start, it is believed that Fulcanelli was a real person! He was an alchemist who worked in early twentieth-century France and he really was part of a secret organisation called the Brothers of Heliopolis. One of the brothers, Eugène Canseliet, declared that Fulcanelli achieved 'The Great Work' some time in the 1920s. This meant Canseliet believed that Fulcanelli not only worked with the Philosopher's Stone, but that he also went on to create the elixir of eternal life.

Shortly after this achievement, Fulcanelli was said to disappear, but the history books suggest that in the 1950s, Canseliet met with Fulcanelli again. What was remarkable about this meeting was that Fulcanelli seemed not to have aged since the 1920s; if anything, he looked younger than before! There are writers who suggest that Fulcanelli also met with Jacques Bergier too, in a gasworks in Paris, and offered him a terrible warning about the progress of science.

The stories about Fulcanelli being hunted by the forerunner of the American CIA are also true. It stands to reason that if it was possible to create an elixir which allowed you to live for ever, a lot of people in positions of power would want to know about it.

But secrecy was the currency of alchemists. Such an incredible discovery would need protecting. So alchemists hid their learning and their discoveries in coded paintings, architecture and writings. I had so much fun exploring some of these secrets in this series.

All the locations the characters visit, across the four books, are based in the real world. Postman's Park, for example, is a beautiful, little-known green space in London – and the Watts Memorial to everyday heroes really exists. The towers and domes, the bridges and tunnels, the statues and the underground locations can all be visited. And if in the story the characters discover unusual features like a scorch mark on a statue of a poet inside St Paul's Cathedral, or a window in the Golden Gallery that looks down to the cathedral floor, then you can be sure that you can really see those features for yourselves. It is my hope that readers will have fun looking more carefully at the world around them, hunting down secrets and symbols hidden in plain sight!

But what of Fulcanelli himself? Did he really reorder the aging process? Is linear reprogramming – like I suggest Jed achieves – actually possible? Those immortal jellyfish in the story really exist too, and they actually can flip back in time to an earlier state of being. Do you think humans ever could do that? And would it be a good idea if we could?

I hope that reading *River of Ink* has raised lots of questions and given you lots to think about and discuss. Maybe you think Jed was wrong to give up the chance to live forever, or maybe you understand exactly why he did. The truth is that alchemists and scientists, philosophers and everyday heroes, have been grappling with these questions for centuries. I hope *River of Ink* has given you an exciting way to think about them for yourself! Thank you so much for coming on the journey of discovery with me.

And maybe next time you look at the 'river of ink'

that washes all around us in our modern lives – with information bombarding us on screens, in paintings and in print – you'll think again about the adventure of life . . . and how the real secret Jed discovered was to embrace that adventure, and truly live each day as fully as you can!

SECRET BREAKERS

Imagine the chance to solve the secret code of the Voynich Manuscript - a puzzle that has defeated adults for centuries.

Together with her new friends, Brodie Bray must break the rules to break the code, at every turn facing terrible danger. For someone is watching them - and will even kill to stop them.

The Secret Breakers series is Dan Brown for kids.
As real codes are being cracked a thrilling adventure unfolds taking the characters across the globe.

www.hldennis.com
www.hodderchildrens.co.uk

Hodder
Children's
Books